The STEAM Series Book 1

Out of the Blu

JENNIFER FISCH-FERGUSON

Out of the Blu

Editor: J. Arthur's Publishing – JAEdits.com

Cover Photo Credits:

Formar Lake: Tri-Crescent Photography – www.tri-crescent.com

Couple: Ashleigh W www.flickr.com/photos/108099221@N02/10751757746/

ISBN: 978-0-9911088-6-2

Table of Contents

Chapter 1

Flora Blu smoothed her hands over the soft cotton, tangerine skirt she wore. The color was a bright, complementary splash against her beautiful, rich mocha coloring. She tried not to be vain, knowing she worked hard to keep her skin smooth, her figure tight, and her brain sharp. Wide, dark brown eyes were gently set in her oval face, and the twinkle of sass reflected in her generous mouth. Her hair was definitely her crowning glory, and she proudly wore it in natural braids. The skirt was a part of the first business suit she had ever owned and came from the newest, Gunnar Deatherage, exclusive, spring collection. She had coveted the rich and vibrant outfit ever since seeing him on the popular, fashion designer show. The suit had been a present from her family for graduating from the University of Flint with both a Master's Degree in Computer Science and Information Systems.

She had been the first in her family to go to college. Flint had been a factory town, housing the Chevrolet plant for years. Over the years, many people had lost jobs when the factories closed down and the city fell on hard times. Even harder still, many people did not understand the necessity of paying for a college education. For generations, people had gone from high school to the factory and made good livings. Adjusting to the new reality of jobs leaving to cheaper, overseas options and management jobs requiring a degree had been an acclimation some people just could not wrap their heads around.

Flora's Momma had seen the shift coming and had drilled into her children the importance and priority of a good education. Flora's Bachelor's Degree in computer science had been celebrated with a block party. She smiled as she remembered the nearly twelve-hour party that had involved a massive barbeque and dancing until the sun rose. By contrast, her Master's degree party involved a quiet dinner with only her parents and two younger brothers in attendance by her request. Flora had news to tell them, and she wasn't quite sure how they would take it and wanted as few witnesses as possible. Despite celebrating her graduation, she had been tense all night, not sure when to share her announcement. No one else seemed to notice her discomfort. Her stomach turned over and over as she waited for the right time to tell them.

"I can't believe the Google down in Ann Arbor offered my baby girl a full-time position," her father had crowed loud enough for everyone around him in the restaurant to hear.

"Daddy, it's not a big deal," she had demurred.

"It most certainly is," he boomed. "First one of our family to graduate and got herself a big-time position at a Fortune 500 company like Google. I'm gonna tell everyone I know."

"Please don't do that," she implored.

"Why wouldn't I? Give me one good reason not to sing your praises."

"I decided not to take the job," she had said. "I am going to open my own business."

Flora shook her head at the rough memory and smoothed her skirt again. She had worked hard to get her small, computer programing business off the ground. Her parents tried to be supportive, but their disappointment about her not taking the other job was still evident. She couldn't mention any concern about not having enough clients without knowing looks passing between them. Many times over the last six months, she wondered about her dedication to staying in the area. It would have been easier to start up a company in Troy or Royal Oak; but Flint was her home, and she was determined to make it. The great news: the rent on her office was cheap, and she won a small, startup business grant for African American women. The bad news: she only had had five clients and needed more steady work. She looked at the calendar with the large, red circle. Rent was due on the fifteenth of each month. She had four more days to get some kind of job before she would have to dig in to her meager savings. The idea of making some cold calls to gain opportunities crossed her mind, but she dismissed it. Flora really didn't enjoy talking on the phone, and the thought of begging for work made her stomach knot.

Her phone chirped and brought her out of her internal, so-to-be funk. She just wanted to work enough to be comfortable, and the reality of not having enough depressed her. She frowned at the number: *For-Mar Nature Preserve and Arboretum.*

"Just what I need," she moaned. "A fundraising call. Sorry, tree huggers, I have nothing for you."

Not only did she not have the money to donate, Flora didn't enjoy nature—at all. She stared at the phone as it chirped again in her hand, wondering if she should answer or just let it go to voicemail. Her business sense won out. She sat up straight, smiled wide, and clicked the green button.

"Flora Blu Program Designs," she said as cheerfully but professionally as she could.

She sat stunned for the next forty-five minutes as a chipper voice, identified as Ginny with a 'G', explained that they needed to hire her to do a recognition program for their box turtles. A shell-pattern recognition program…for turtles. However, they had received a grant from Michigan State University and were offering her almost ten thousand dollars for her work. Flora accepted the job without having any idea of how she would fulfill the order, because with that kind of money she would make rent—for the year and then some. Flora sat back with a smile and knew that it would be a great, community connection and might even lead to more work from the Genesee County Park system. But before her meeting with their specialist, she needed to read up on turtles.

Flora stretched her arms high above her head. She had thought that researching turtles would have taken an hour at best. Two hours later, she was still reading and rather amazed at the complexity of the reptiles. That had been the first thing she had learned. Flora had always thought the little creatures were amphibians, but she learned quickly that turtle's metamorphosize, have shells, and had scaly skin. Those were just some of the qualifications. At the end of her research, Flora came up with a hard won conclusion: She would have to venture out to For-Mar prior to the meeting. She really needed to take a look at these turtles in their displays, so she would at least sound like she knew what she was doing. She sighed. Nature just really wasn't her thing. Still, the payday wasn't something she was about to turn down.

Before she could really think about all of the insects and bugs and other nature-related things she would encounter, Flora hopped in her car and started the journey out to For-Mar. She passed under the welcome sign and smiled at the flowers along the side of the driveway. Someone had taken a lot of time and put a lot of effort into making it so beautiful, and she was amazed at the riot of colors. She parked in the last space in a jam-packed parking lot. There were four school buses, a couple of church vans, and a lot of cars.

"Wow. Who would've thought this place was so popular?" Flora said. "I've lived here my whole life and never visited. Of course it's a nature preserve and that's not really my thing."

She smiled and shook her head at herself. Her habit of talking out loud to herself when nervous would probably get her in trouble someday. Despite the communication courses in college, old habits die hard, but at least she was aware of them. She took a deep breath and prepared to meet the creatures making her rent.

She congratulated herself for having taken the time to change out of her skirt and into a soft pair of grey, cotton slacks, a lime green, silk, V-neck top, and practical, tan wedges to complete her outfit. Despite being in the sticks, she still needed to look professional. Flora walked across the driveway and to the visitor's center. It bustled with activity, and she pressed her lips together. She had no desire to walk through the squirming mass of kids to get to the information desk, but she had no choice. All she needed was a good idea of what the little buggers looked like up close so she could write the appropriate program.

"Excuse me. I need to see the turtles," she called out to the young lady sitting behind the desk.

She got a smile and a "one-moment" finger as the lady handed out maps and pointed harried-looking parents to a row of explorer backpacks on a wall. A small flurry of arms and legs and their parents rushed past Flora, and she stepped closer to the desk. She could see the name Ginny on the name tag and smiled again at her. Ginny-with-a-G was more petite than she had sounded over the phone, but she was efficiently handing out maps, pointing out directions, and gathering up two groups to go out. Once the people were on their way to a nature adventure, she turned and smiled at Flora.

"The turtles are out back," Ginny said.

"Right through this door? Are they in a special part of the center?"

"No," Ginny laughed. "Just follow the path behind the center. It's pretty easy to spot."

"Outside?" Flora asked.

"Yes, we keep our ponds outside here," Ginny said with a grin. "It should be pretty empty right now. The last tour took the long way around. Aside from you and a few families, it should be clear for another ninety minutes."

Flora nodded her head and went back outside. She easily found the path and grimaced when she saw the dirt and leaves that covered it. Her tan wedges would definitely need to be scrubbed after her little venture. She stumbled a bit when the land sloped and resisted cursing because she knew children were in the area. She wished for a handkerchief to mop her brow and felt a trickle of sweat run down between her breasts. She stared in amazement at the pond directly in front of her. It was surrounded by weeds and a dirt walkway. Across the pond seemed to be a little, treehouse observatory, and she could see a dock to the left. She could see a few turtles sunning themselves on a half-sunken log, and all of a sudden Flora wanted to cry. She could feel the money slip out of her hands as the enormity of the job she had taken settled in.

These weren't turtles in a display pond at the visitor's center, like her brain had allowed her to imagine during her phone conversation with Ginny. They were out in the wild, in the water, and pretty darn inaccessible as far as Flora was concerned. Still, she did not plan to give up. She walked, carefully, down the path to the docks and stared. Two small boys lay at the end, their faces mere inches from the water, and laughed as they pointed to things she could not see. She watched as they unpacked a magnifying glass, a small, flat disk, and a measuring cup from the backpack. In a few seconds, they had scooped a cup of water into the dish and looked through the glass, exploring it.

"That's pretty cool," Flora said. "It's nice they give them all the tools to work with."

The words rang in the air, and she grimaced. Unfortunately, she was not alone and found herself engaged in conversation with a mother who probably hadn't had adult conversation all day.

"Yes, those backpacks are amazing. They pack up field guides, animal and bird guides, along with some equipment that let the kids explore. It's the best free activity around and has the benefit of keeping them occupied for hours."

"It sounds like a great way to keep your kids busy. Not to mention they're learning something useful."

"Yeah, this place is full of awesome classes and workshops," the young mother said. "Okay, boys, time to move on."

The boys quickly scooped everything up and ran off the deck with ease. Flora, on the other hand, eyed the deck like it was her imminent doom and wondered how sturdy it was. She stepped onto the wood and waited for it to sway and pitch. It didn't, and she gave a silent laugh of relief. Flora stepped carefully as she walked down the dock. She made the mental note to wear flats the next time she had to be there.

"I swear it feels like I am walking the plank," she muttered.

She knelt down and peered into the water, surprised that it wasn't murky and gross looking. She could see fish of various sizes swimming and also some turtles. She smiled, watching them swim and move about freely. She peered closer and was surprised to see quite a few, now that she knew what she was looking for. She was delighted to see so many baby turtles. According to her research, most of the eggs would have been laid in July, so she was happy to see so many had hatched and made it to the pond. Flora had been amazed to learn that mothers would lay eggs somewhere in moist sand in a sunny spot with the expectation that the babies would break out of their shells and, somehow, find their way to the pond. Of course, this was if the raccoons, snakes, and other egg-loving creatures didn't get them first.

She sat watching the turtles for a while. The sun was nice and warm, and the turtles kept moving from logs to the water and back. She had tried to count how many turtles were in the pond, but she realized there was no way for her to keep track. She would need a linked camera system to gather enough photos of all of them to begin categorizing the patterns for recognition. Flora tried not to weep as she felt a good portion of her payday reallocating itself to purchasing equipment. She pushed back up onto her feet and wobbled as the blood rushed back through her legs.

"No falling now," she told herself. "That pond is full of turtle poo, and I have no desire to swim in it."

She weaved her way back down the dock, and taking the path to her right, she moved toward the observation space. Flora sighed in relief when she stood at the base of the platform and saw steps leading up to the space. She had almost convinced herself that she would be shimmying up the tree to get there. She climbed the steps and stood in the small, wooden room, looking over the pond and trying to calculate all the parameters she would need for her program.

Hairs stood up on the back of her neck, and she became aware that another body shared the space she was in. The smallest creak of the boards had alerted her to someone entering. She bit the inside of her bottom lip to make sure she wouldn't scream, unless she really needed to. Flora turned slowly to see who had joined her. The preparations to make noise and alert Ginny to her distress withered away as she looked into the most mesmerizing caramel eyes she had ever seen.

"Sorry for disturbing you," he said. "I left my field journal up here, and I need to enter the data from my notes."

He reached around her to grab something, but all she could concentrate on was the heat that scorched her skin as his arm passed over it. Flora stood shock-still, saying nothing, because she had the embarrassing desire to reach out and caress the well-toned bicep as it went by her. She tried to smile, to give him some sort of response, but he just nodded at her and walked away.

"Holy hell," she breathed out after she could no longer hear his feet going down the steps. "Do all nature lovers look like that?"

Flora was certain the heat that flushed through her body had nothing to do with the August sun. She stood a few more moments in the observation room, reliving her short encounter, and then, shaking her head, she walked back to the parking lot. She still had a lot to figure out about how to get a recognition pattern fluid enough to capture all the nuances of the shell patterns. She was almost to her car when she realized that Ginny might be able to give her information on what types of turtles she would be dealing with.

An hour later, Flora was in possession of a turtle shell—minus the turtle—and a head stuffed full of turtle facts. She carried the shell in a plastic bag between her fingertips. She made a mental note to stop by the drug store on the way home to get some plastic gloves. At least fifty pairs and the strongest sanitizer they carried. This was going to be a long project if they expected her to touch the nature.

Chapter 2

Gregory Bell walked through the winding trails at For-Mar, enjoying the afternoon heat. His six-foot-two frame moved through the foliage with ease. He barely paid any attention to the landscape around him; he could traverse the trails blind, if need be. The preserve had become his home a year before, and he spent a lot of time walking around the 383-acre park. With the spike in temperature, he was glad to have shorn his soft, dark curls into a neat, polished fade. Generally in the summer, he just went for a buzz cut, but his barber talked him into a change. A few smug comments about his abstinent lifestyle of late had made their mark, and he agreed to the new style. He shook his head at how his friends would shame him for not pursuing every pretty woman he came across. They did miss the point of keeping things separate. He loved his job, hanging out with his friends, and his privacy. He just didn't need them to intertwine and cause issues.

It's not that he was avoiding dating. He just hadn't found anyone interesting as of late. Even still, he found nothing wrong with being alone. He had learned to embrace the silence and calm, and the last few times he had gone out, the females were just too chaotic for him. He shook his head at his thoughts. He had been born and raised in Flint, a city boy. More than a few people he had grown up with were more than surprised that he had gone to work for a nature preserve. Gregory had done more than that; he had gotten his degree in wildlife biology and spent two years in Alabama getting his graduate degree in Testudinology.

He had planned his education around returning to Flint and working at For-Mar. He was the Director of Educational Programs for local area, school-aged programs, and he got to drive the Turtle Mobile. The generous funding For-Mar received made it easy to create new and innovative programs that drew a lot of local and sometimes state-wide interest. He had begun to volunteer at the preserve while in high school and made sure he could return after graduate school. He had made a comfortable life for himself and figured someday he would have a partner. He just didn't feel like there was a countdown that he had to contend with.

His dark, caramel eyes darted over to a flurry of movement, and he smiled at the squirrels defending their territories. They broke his reverie, and he ran over the schedule he had for the day when a bright shock of green caught his attention. He had been walking up to the visitor's center to prepare for the next group of kids to take on a nature walk, when he had seen a very beautiful, very out-of-place woman kneeling on the dock. He watched her nose wrinkle as she smiled, laughed, and watched the turtles in the pond. When she stood, he was certain she was going to plunge into the pond as she wobbled on her ridiculous footwear. Intrigued at what could have possibly brought her out to the pond, he couldn't help but follow her as she walked to the observation point.

Gregory was impressed that she didn't kill herself walking up the steps to the small, observation hut. He watched her stare out the window with a tiny frown wrinkling her lips. She sighed deeply, apparently working out some kind of problem as she stared out over the pond. He walked over and slowly made his way up closer to her and could tell the moment she sensed him. She turned cautiously, and he watched her throat constrict as she looked him over. She said nothing as he gave his flimsy excuse and grabbed the field book that was housed there. As his arm moved past her body, he couldn't believe that such a light touch caused him to react and continued to get more turned on by the second. He walked down the steps and hid in the bushes around the corner. He watched the woman leave, watching her until she crested the small hill. She was beautiful. His body still reacted to their brief encounter. He shook his head as he made it up to the center. He stayed in the backyard until he saw her leave.

"Ginny, who was the city girl?" he asked as he entered the building.

"Our new turtle specialist," she said.

"So why wasn't I informed about another specialist coming in? I created this program and I don't need an outsider messing with my pond" he said. "Besides, did you see her? She looked like a cover model, not a biologist."

"She is making the database," Ginny said with a smirk. "Relax. She isn't stealing your job. She is just cataloguing the turtles."

"Oh. Well, I guess that is okay, then," he said. "A database for what?"

"Really, Gregory, you were the one who suggested the idea," Ginny said, shoving a clipboard at him. "I will give you all the gory details later. Your group just pulled up."

Gregory nodded and, walking into the staff room, grabbed his backpack. He felt stupid for forgetting about the whole plan to have someone come in and create a database. He had read an article about the Zoo in Southwest Portland, Oregon doing something similar, had suggested it to the preserve director, written a grant, and promptly forgotten about it. He took a long drink of water and got into the headspace to deal with his next group. The boys from the summer program were between eleven and thirteen—a hot mess of hormones, growth spurts, and end-of-summer boredom. He knew that he would have to keep them moving and exploring to make sure they didn't get into trouble. He walked out and greeted the harried-looking chaperone, and with one loud whistle he commanded the attention of the twelve boys.

"Welcome to For-Mar Nature Preserve. Today we are going to hike all seven miles of the amazing trails we have here and create some field journals of the best looking bugs nature has to offer. My name is Gregory, and I will be your guide to the outdoors. Fall in line, and let's get started."

He smiled as the boys lined up with no incident. He hoped it was a sign of how the day would progress. He handed out their backpacks and water bottles and rattled off the few rules they would have to follow. The chaperones gave him a knowing smile, and in a short five minutes they were on the trails. With the sun bright and a light breeze, it was going to be a great afternoon.

Gregory gave a stress-relieving sigh as he walked into his house. The blessed silence was beautiful to his ears. After a full four hours with the boys, he was ready not to hear another voice…forever. The kids weren't bad; they were just kids. Full of energy, getting into every damn thing, throwing dirt and leaves, and trying to climb, conquer, or destroy things. In short—boys. Thankfully, no bones had been broken, despite how many attempted to follow squirrels up the trees. He wondered how the chaperones could do it all the time. Gregory figured they drank. A lot.

The journey had started out with stick wars, meaning every boy had found some kind of stick—the bigger the better—and began to use it as a sword. Mile two found the boys utterly bored and straying randomly off the paths, but the warning of rattle snakes had taken care of that wanderlust. Mile four gave them the reprieve of a lunch break, and while he tried to explain how different herbs found around them were used in their everyday foods, a small group had snuck off and found and eaten berries. Blackberries, thankfully, but still the talk about poison berries and forced, mass gagging had ensued. Mile seven was the worst. The boys were tired, bored, and had sore muscles. The heat of the day made them sweat. They had run out of water, and the flying bugs swarmed around them. The whining at top volume all the way back to the center made him acutely aware how each boy felt about nature, bugs, and him.

Gregory shook his head clear of his job, and after about three minutes of standing in his house, he decided that he needed some water therapy. He walked out the back door and down the small, sloping hill. He pulled off his shirt as he walked towards the lake. He stood at the end of his dock, took off his shoes, and shucked off his pants. He dove into the clear, blue water and emerged with a cleansing sigh. He swam with sure strokes out to the raft in the middle of the lake and back to shore again. After a couple dozen laps, he pulled himself up on to the empty raft and lay back. It was quiet but still warm at the end of summer.

Gregory lay out, watching the few clouds skitter across the sky. He lay contentedly until his stomach reminded him that lunch had been twelve whining boys ago. He slipped into the water and took his time swimming back. He walked into his house to pull on a pair of shorts and flip-flops, before starting his grill for dinner. He had walked back down to the lake to check his fish traps, when he felt a pair of eyes staring at him. He grabbed a couple bluegills and took them back to his deck.

"Tess," he said, acknowledging the eyes that had watched him.

"We need to talk, Gregory," she said.

Gregory watched her unfold herself from his patio chair. She stood before him and tension rolled off her in waves he could feel. They stood in a silent stare-off, for a few moments, until he heard the coals pop. He walked over to his station near the grill and started scaling the fish.

"If you want to join me for dinner, I am going to need more fish," he said. "Stop acting like you are a stranger here."

He made it a point to cut the head off his two fish before he looked back at her. Her lips thinned, but she walked down the small slope to the lake and went to the trap. Tess was a beautiful woman, no doubt, but also a handful he didn't plan to deal with. She was tall at six feet, and her skin was a rich chocolate, not as dark as his, but smooth and supple. She had clearly defined muscles, and her long locks framed her round face. Dark eyes, a straight nose, and a wide mouth finished the exotic look. At least, it was exotic when not tightened in irritation. She returned and all but glared at him as she held out two, wriggling bluegills.

"Do I need to clean my own fish, too?"

"I got it," Gregory said, smart enough not to hand her a knife with the mood she was in.

"About that talk?" she queried as he scaled and filleted her fish.

"Okay, let's talk," he said, tossing the fish in seasoning and putting them on the grill.

"We need to talk about us," Tess said, folding her long frame back into the patio chair.

Gregory walked to the opposite side of his deck and grabbed some peppers and zucchini out of his garden box. He started slicing the vegetables and putting them on the grill. He finished his task before looking back at Tess.

"Tess, I am all good with your decision," he said. "You made it very clear that our *friendliness* this winter was just a temporary situation. Just what is there for us to talk about? Was there more you wanted me to know? I am okay with us just being neighbors."

"Are you sure? I saw the looks you were giving me and Rex last night."

"Don't read more into it. I didn't snarl or glower at you. I just happened to look over when you were laughing. I'm happy you have found someone that you like," he said.

"Okay. I don't want things to get uncomfortable."

Gregory stared at her. She sat calm and still for about ten seconds and then began to fidget.

"What more do you want me to say?" he asked her.

"I just need to make sure you are okay," Tess said.

"You're here for dinner, aren't you?" Gregory asked and tended the food on the grill. "I am okay. We are both adults, and I expect us to continue to treat each other with respect. I haven't ignored you nor spoken badly about you to others. I don't even think we have been awkward with each other. So don't worry. I will not snarl or pick fights with your next guy. Just like I wouldn't expect you to act out with any woman I date."

"Well, if you're okay," she said shortly.

He watched Tess walk into his house and grab plates and utensils. Her behavior signaled that, perhaps she didn't like his calm demeanor. He really had been okay when she called things off. During the winter, it had been a fun distraction to have her attentions. Michigan had decided to open up and give them an amazing three feet of snow over one weekend in December alone. Meaning a lot of everything had shut down. Just when the plows had the streets clear and things were back to normal, January came and brought many more feet. Tess had come over one night when the power had knocked out, asking to stay in his spare room since her generator had broken. She didn't leave for two more months.

"Really, Tess, we were both aware of what it was," he said.

She handed him the plates, and they sat at the outside table, eating. Gregory was fine with the quiet; he had no need to fill the silence with meaningless chatter. Tess ate quickly and stood abruptly, disturbing the birdsong. He watched her rise and pace a moment. She looked at him and he returned the look with a steady gaze. He slowly ate his food, not wanting to say anything else. No amount of words would change the end of their relationship.

"I think I will go for now," she said. "I do mean it, Gregory. I want us to be okay."

He smiled at her, realizing she might be having more issues than he about calling off their tryst. Perhaps she had wanted more, but followed his lead? He wouldn't make a relationship out of nothing. In fact, he realized that his body hadn't reacted to her through their entire dinner. It had another woman in mind.

"It's fine," he said. "Go on. Tomorrow, you get to cook."

That was apparently what she had needed to hear, and she left with a smile. He watched her walk across the yard to her home and inside. He cleaned up dinner and then sat on the deck, nursing a cold beer. He watched the moon rise, fat and yellow in the sky. One more until it would be a full moon for three days. His skin itched and rippled. The need to run in the moonlight struck him hard. He peered up again and took a deep breath. It gave shadow to the trees and the few other houses around the lake. The song of crickets lulled him into relaxation, and he watched the spiraling flight of bats until the mosquitos made him retreat to his room. He took off his shorts and climbed into the cool sheets on his bed. His mind wandered back to the woman he hadn't quite met in the observatory and hoped he would get a chance to find out who she was.

Chapter 3

Flora woke up after dreaming all night about turtles. The darn things had plagued her for a full two weeks as she read and studied and read even more about the little creatures. She looked over at her nightstand where the shell sat. She swore it mocked her somehow, and she couldn't wait to take the thing back to the center.

"I am going to be forever haunted by these damn things," she muttered.

She forced herself into a sitting position and reached out for her tablet. With a push of three buttons, the coffee maker started, the air conditioning unit sprang to life, and the shower started running. There were distinct advantages to being a programmer. She walked into a perfectly hot shower a few moments later, and while she soaped up, her brain tried to figure out how she could spend less money. She didn't want to have to build a server for the nature preserve, but she needed some way to keep the captured information.

With her shower done and a mug of coffee in her hands, Flora sat on her floor, trying to meditate. Had someone told her two years ago that yoga and meditation would become her daily practice, she would have scoffed. She didn't mind a good workout; she had an intimate relationship with an elliptical machine. But yoga? She never had any intention of putting her leg around her neck. That was before graduate school. Half way through her first semester, her favorite teacher told her that if she didn't find something aside from work and school, she would crash and burn. He had suggested yoga, and to her credit, Flora did not laugh in his face. Two weeks later, when she cried for two hours over an A- on her paper, she reconsidered. Her first yoga class had included a guided meditation at the end, and her life snapped back into focus. She had been doing both practices ever since. She finished her first cup of coffee, and as she began her gentle stretching, she connected to her body and soul. It was about an hour later, as she held downward dog for an extra thirty seconds, that the answer caught up to her in a rush.

"If I use a variation of the Voronoi diagram, I can create character points and finesse the recognition. All I need are a few more cameras."

She had learned that Eastern box turtles are characterized by their highly domed top shell, called the carapace, which were brightly colored with a middorsal keel down the center. Carapace color varied greatly between individuals, containing smudges, streaks, blotches, or mottling that could be yellow, red, orange, or brown. Even better, each shell was as unique as a fingerprint, so creating a program to identify and catalogue the shell patterns would be as easy as facial recognition, and then it would just feed into her database program.

Flora felt much better and quickly got dressed. She needed to go shopping. Hours later, she came back with her new telemetry equipment. She was giddy with excitement and was even looking forward to going out to For-Mar to set up her station. She rushed out of her car and up the four flights of stairs to her apartment. She needed to search through her spare tech drawer to find the parts she needed. After lugging a boxful down to the car, she was ready to get to work. She glanced down as she buckled her seat belt and was glad she had changed out of her gray, cotton trousers. Despite being a job, she was not going to wreck one of the three pair of nice work pants she owned. She hoped that she would have enough money left over from the job to add another business outfit to her collection. While carefully considering her options, she decided to wear her boat shoes. They were cute, and she had only had the chance to wear them twice the summer before. The pink and black pattern made her reconsider her outfit, and she decided to change into a black, denim jumper with a pink, sleeveless, button-down top. She was halfway down the stairs when she remembered the turtle shell. And the plastic gloves.

"You, little dude, do not need another sleepover at my house," she said, snatching it up between her thumb and finger.

Empty or not, she had no desire to touch it more than necessary. She tossed it into a plastic bag. Finally satisfied, Flora again walked down to her car and began the trip to For-Mar. She was driving down the drive to the visitor center when her phone rang. It was her best friend, Shonise; she pressed the button on her steering wheel.

"Yes, beautiful?" she asked as she greeted her friend.

"I think you need to play hooky today and come with me down to Detroit," Shonise said.

"No can do, sister," Flora said with a grin.

"But…Fishbone's," Shonise tempted.

"I've got a new job, and I cannot skip out this early." She lowered the volume as the happy shrieking nearly pierced her eardrums. After promising to meet her friend at The White Horse later that evening, she hung up and parked in the semi-circle drive close to the center. She went into the center to ask Ginny where to put her equipment. Ginny wasn't at the desk, and the center was very quiet, compared to her experience the day before. She poked her head around into the rooms and saw no one.

"Can I help you?"

Flora let out a shrieking *eep* and whirled around. Heat bloomed in her cheeks for making the sound. She looked at who had asked the question, and her breath caught in her throat. It was the man from the observation station. And he looked as delicious as she had remembered. A few minutes passed before she realized she was still standing there, staring at him.

"I was…I mean, I am trying…" she mumbled out loud. "Well, that was fun."

Flora took a deep breath and then extended her hand.

"Hi. I'm Flora Blu. I was hired for the turtle shell recognition project here, and I need to know where I can store my equipment," she said.

She almost missed the man's name when he grabbed her hand in greeting. A tingle started as his fingers rested on her wrist. His large hand was warm but calloused and easily enveloped hers. He pumped hers gently, and the touch made her stomach flutter. She swallowed against a suddenly dry throat and put a smile on her face, hoping she did not look like an idiot. Her mind quickly replayed what it heard him say.

"Gregory. I'm certain you can use the staff room," he said. "It's right past the main desk."

"Thanks."

She nodded and backed away from him until her shoulder hit the door frame. She blushed again as she turned around and was thankful when she made it back to her car without tripping or falling. Flora was certain that her awkward first impression would go down in history as her worst. Popping her trunk, she was sad that she had not brought a wagon to carry all the boxes. She had lugged the first large box to the edge of her trunk and tried to balance it as she got ready to lift it. It wobbled and threatened to take everything with it. She grabbed the topmost box and sighed as the rest settled.

"Do you need any help?"

Flora eeped again and turned to see Gregory about a foot away from her. The boxes fell back into her car.

"I did not even hear you come out," she said, trying to compose herself.

"You seemed fairly involved with staring into your trunk," he said with an easy smile.

Flora fell into the dimple that appeared on his left cheek. She stood there a few more seconds until he grabbed the box from her hands.

"Let me help you with those."

"You could at least make sound when you move," she muttered to his retreating backside.

Although, she admired said backside until he walked into the center. She hastily grabbed a smaller box and followed him in. They walked back out in silence for a final trip to get her remaining equipment. She set the box on the table and smiled.

"Thanks for the help, Gregory," she said. "I really appreciate your kindness."

"My pleasure, Flora-Blu," he said.

His voice was like slow-melting dark chocolate as he combined her name. She began to pull out pieces and set them on the table, trying to find the monopods she had just bought. She hoped it would calm the riot of thoughts she had about the man, and it kept her trembling hands busy. She had not been on a date in over a year—a travesty, if Shonise were to be believed. But grad school, as well as her job, had not left a lot of time to be involved with a relationship. Her last experience had not been the best. Daryl's idea of a good time involved her reprogramming games for his system so he could either cheat to win the game or make enhanced avatars. After a while, she realized just how much he took her skills for granted. Of course, she also learned how passionate he was for the games and the people he played with. Despite her horrid experience, it didn't mean that she didn't find men attractive anymore. It just meant it had been a long time since she had wanted one.

"If I made sound, I would never have gotten to see your pretty blush."

Her head snapped up, and her eyes met his. He held her eyes for a moment then nodded and walked out of the room. She couldn't believe that he had heard her. What if she had made a much more suggestive statement? Flora stood there looking at the spot where he had been and then scolded herself.

"Get it together, Flora. You are acting like a silly, simpering teenager. Yes, he is handsome and lovely to look at. Those eyes are amazing and just stop it. You're here on a job, and lusting after employees is a good way to get fired," she said under her breath.

She grabbed a sketchpad and a pencil and walked out to the pond. She needed to get some measurements and plot how to best get coverage of the pond. It was larger than she remembered as she walked around the circumference. She shook her head at her own folly of buying equipment before having her details. Part of that was the excitement of shopping for new technology with a decent budget. She figured she should be able to capture all the turtles if she left her cameras for about a week and then came back to change angles for another week.

Flora wrinkled her nose at the idea of having to come back out every other day to change the batteries, but it had to be done. She doubted the turtles would agree to line up and sit for her while she took pictures of them all. She sighed and made a few sketches—very rudimentary sketches—and then made her way back to the center. Now she just had to get the cameras in place, and she could call it a day.

Flora took her ten monopods and walked back out to the lake. She tried to figure out the best place to put the pods and realized she was going to have to test just how deep the lake was.

"I am so not into non-pool water," she said. "This would be so much easier if they just had the turtles in a big, glass tank. This is why we have zoos."

She walked out on the dock and had a fleeting idea of throwing the monopod like a javelin into the center of the lake. She giggled just a bit at the notion but doubted she actually had any javelin-throwing skills. She carefully sat on the sun-warmed wood and inched closer to the edge of the dock. She leaned over just a bit and pushed the pole into the water. Fish swam away in terror as she made it go down as far as she could. She grimaced as her hand went into the water and continued to make faces as it took up to her elbow to get the pod down far enough. Flora stood up and shook off her arm. She had the notion that the center of the pond was going to be too deep, so she planned to place her cameras around the circumference. She walked to the right and found herself with a problem she had not anticipated. To gain access back to the water line, she would have to walk through some weedy areas. Weeds that probably had bugs. Flora straightened her shoulders, determined to get the hard part of the job done, and pressed through the weeds. She moaned as lukewarm water sloshed over her boat shoes. She hadn't thought that the weeds would hide water. Slimy, nasty, non-chlorinated, swamp water.

"Well, too late now," she huffed. "One would think that since these stupid things are called boat shoes they would actually keep your feet dry from the water. Let's just get the damn things in the water."

Flora walked a bit deeper and placed the second pod in the water. Of course, this one didn't go under the water, and she had to wade into the pond even further to get to a position where she could submerge her equipment. She wanted to curse like a sailor but didn't figure it would actually help anything. She sloshed in the water to her next position. The heat from the sun reminded her that she would need to bring a hat when she came to change the batteries and upload the pictures.

Her plan was brilliant, if Flora did say so herself. She had bought ten digital cameras that had an operating system and Bluetooth capability. She hacked the program and gave it a new set of directives to make her life easier. She set up the command for the cameras to snap a picture whenever the sensor detected the Voronoi diagram shape. This way she would get only the turtles, instead of everything else that was in the pond. Creatures that she didn't want to think about as she stood ankle-deep in their midst.

Flora made her way slowly around the pond, happy with the progress she made. Her self-imposed goal of finishing before she left spurred her on even faster. She had to navigate through weeds and sticks to get her monopods into their proper positions. It was harder than she thought it would be. She finally was on her last monopod and grunted as she shoved it into the muck at the bottom.

"Who knew that the stupid things wouldn't just sink? And why isn't it a nice, sandy bottom? Stupid, scummy pond water source."

As sweat trickled from her brow and down her back, she cursed herself for having forgotten her handkerchief again. No doubt, after her time at For-Mar, she would be freckled, and her skin would be a hot mess from all the sweating. But it was okay. After she was done, she would be meeting up with Shonise and probably a few of her other girls at the White Horse to have a few drinks. She was excited that she finally had some awesome news to share with her friends. Much like her family, they didn't understand why she would give up such a big job. All but Shonise, who had her back and loudly and proudly let everyone know that Flora working for herself was amazing. She smiled again and made plans to buy the first few rounds of drinks for her BFF.

As she stood thinking of which drink she would start with, something bit at her ankles. Flora shrieked, screamed, and began flailing and dancing around. She wasn't sure which direction it had come from, so she didn't know how to escape it. She looked down but saw nothing, except long, green strands of seaweed. She tried to calm herself so she could make a plan of escape. She stood still for a few moments, and the nibbling sensation came back. Flashes of red darted away as she moved.

This time, Flora didn't care if she had to walk through slime and muck. She ran out of the pond, lifting her legs as high up as they would go, shrieking and wailing the whole time. She shook by the time she got to shore. She took huge, gulping breaths and examined her legs.

Flora jumped out of her skin when a hand touched her shoulder and then groaned when she heard the words.

"Are you okay, Flora Blu?"

Chapter 4

Gregory couldn't believe what he had just seen. Flora wading ankle-deep in the pond for reasons unknown to him. Then, all of a sudden, she started dancing around and screaming like she had been attacked. The snakes sometimes swam in the pond, but he couldn't imagine one getting close enough to bite her. He rushed over to where she was and found her shaking, but no obvious marks were on her legs. Her beautiful, smooth, long legs.

"Are you okay, Flora Blu?" he asked.

She jumped as he touched her shoulder and then turned to look at him, her eyes wide and lips pressed in to a thin line. She trembled but tried to compose herself.

"Something bit at me in there," she said, pointing an accusing finger at the pond.

Gregory leaned over and examined her legs up close.

"I don't see any blood or puncture marks," he said, leaning down to run a hand over her soft and shapely legs. "The fish probably took a nibble at you."

"Fish?" she squeaked. "You really have piranhas in there?"

"No. Those are only found in the Amazon basin," he said with a smile meant to reassure and felt her tremble. "Let's get you back to the center. What were you doing out in the pond, anyhow? We do not allow any swimming."

He guided her with a gentle hand on her back, but really he wished he could have kept stroking her legs. Gregory took a breath and put himself in check. He was taking advantage of the fact that she had freaked out over a few minnows nipping at her.

"I was setting up my monopods so I could get pictures of all of the turtles," she said. "This way I can create the database of how many unique turtles you have. That's what they hired me for."

"I have pictures of the turtles, if you want to use them," he offered.

"Thank you, Gregory, but I am going to need pictures of every single one."

He could hear the dismissal in her voice and didn't push it. The poor woman had just been attacked by minnows. He could hear her breathing calm the further she got from the pond. He figured he would need to help her gather the data over the next few weeks. Flora was adorably unknowledgeable about turtles and quite frankly knew nothing about nature photography. And as any good park ranger would, Gregory planned to offer his services to her.

"How about I help you wash the pond water off?"

"Um, okay. You aren't going to spray me with a hose are you?"

He chuckled. "No, I have a basin and a washcloth."

He moved her quickly back to the center and into the staff longue. Thankfully, it was empty and, according to the schedule on the fridge, it would be for the next few hours. He grabbed the supplies and motioned for her to sit. Gregory smiled at Flora as she watched his preparations. He handed her a bottle of water he had grabbed and then using his utility knife, sliced a lemon into halves and dropped them into the water in the basin.

"A lemon?" she asked, raising an eyebrow.

"They are good for a foot massage," he said. "After your terror by minnow, I figured you could use some relaxation."

"It will have to be damn good to erase that terror," she said, raising the water bottle as exclamation. "Why don't you warn people about those flesh eating fish?"

"No one is supposed to go into the pond," he chuckled.

As she sipped the water, he slowly washed the pond water off her legs. Then he dipped the washcloth in the basin, held it above her knee, and let the water drip down her calf and run over her foot. He watched her eyes widen at the sensation and repeated the technique on the other leg. Two more times, he allowed water to drip down over her skin, and then grabbing half a lemon, he rubbed it over her feet one at a time. They were already soft, but the acid in the lemon would extract toxins from her system and help her relax even more. He continued the massage and looked up at her. Flora had slouched just a bit with the careful touches to her feet.

Gregory put the lemon back in the water, slowly lifted one of her feet, and began a slow rotation of her ankle, clockwise and then counterclockwise. The soft sigh coming from her made the hairs on his arms rise up. He swallowed hard and began to work the other foot. Her breathing hitched as he switched from her ankles to her toes, rotating them, pushing and pulling on them gently. He watched her breathe deeply and lose herself in the sensations as her legs and feet relaxed under his ministrations.

He rubbed his thumbs back and forth over the soles of her feet and pushed in deeply to work the pressure points. His stomach clenched as a low, husky moan poured out of her lips, and Gregory started to wish he had not started this little seduction at the very public visitor's center. However, he reasoned they weren't going to be disrupted, so he might as well finish what he had started.

Directly beneath the ball of her foot, he began to move his thumbs in semicircles, working back and forth horizontally. He then worked to heighten the sensations even more by placing his thumbs on opposite sides of her sole and slid them toward each other and to the opposite side of her foot. He could feel the tension melt as he pushed his thumbs into the soft flesh. She let out a deep, lustful, earthy groan, and Gregory paused a moment as pictures of other ways to help her make those enticing sounds flooded his mind. He watched Flora slide a bit more down in the chair, thinking how easy it would be to lean in and taste each moan coming from her mouth.

Instead, he interlaced his fingers, resting them on the top of her foot, and placed his thumbs against her sole. He slid his thumbs up and down over the whole foot, applying pressure. He then switched to the outside of her ankle, found where the muscle met the bone, and ran his thumb along this line all the way up her shin, applying slight pressure. He could imagine moving that leg up enough to lie across his shoulder and…his eyes snapped to her face. Thankfully, Flora's eyes were blissfully closed, and she couldn't read his thoughts.

At this point, Gregory knew he needed some distance. He was too turned on to hide it and needed to calm himself. He quickly finished his impromptu massage, dried her ankles and feet, and put them down onto a soft towel.

"Is that better?" he asked as he moved to the sink to hide his beginning show of arousal.

"Yes," she breathed.

He would be at that damn sink forever if she kept making sounds like that.

"I think you might want to invest in a pair of galoshes if you are going to be working in the pond," he said.

"Thank you, Gregory," she said. "How about tomorrow I help you set up your equipment?" he asked.

"That would be amazing," Flora said.

He was surprised when she actually clapped her hands as she said it.

"Once I get the gear set up, it should move much more quickly."

Gregory didn't like the sound of that. He wanted to see more of her, not help her leave. It had taken him watching her visit a few times before he actually approached her, and he wasn't going to waste any more time. He finally was calm enough to stop rinsing the washcloth and turned to face her. Her cheeks and nose were clearly sunburned, but her eyes were bright and excited. She kept nibbling on her bottom lip, just the right corner.

"Remember a hat and galoshes tomorrow," he said, more brusquely than he intended.

"Right," she said, not noticing. "And I'll have to bring my tablet to make sure the Bluetooth connection is strong enough and also try two different types of batteries to see which last the longest and—oh, never mind. You probably don't want to hear me ramble on about all the stuff I need to bring."

He nodded and held out a hand, and she grinned as he helped her rise. She walked by his side out of the center and to her car. She was quiet, probably finishing her lists in her head, but held on to his hand as she walked. Gregory wanted to laugh at the animated expressions on her face as she figured out whatever is was that she thought over.

"Do you play poker?" he joked.

"No. I mean, I did once, but they thought I was cheating or that I already knew how. I mean, it's just numbers and probability," she frowned. "Not my fault they were so bad with numbers."

He couldn't help it. Gregory threw his head back and laughed hard. She was so earnest in her upset, and he knew she had no idea why the other players were so disgusted with her play. She grinned at him and got in her car.

"I will see you tomorrow," she said and then drove away.

He chuckled as he walked back past the center and to the trails. She was the most interesting person he had met in a while, not to mention the pure chaos she caused with his hormones. He decided after their work date, he would ask her for an evening and see where it took him. He was lost in plans for what he could introduce her to, as he walked through the trails. He couldn't wait to show her some of the lesser used trails around the reserve, and with any luck, the turtleheads would be blooming. The perfect flower for the woman who had been brought in to create a database for his turtles.

Later that evening, Gregory walked through the woods towards an opening. A large bonfire reached upwards and sparked into the dark night and hosted a couple dozen people. He smiled and greeted his friends and brothers as he entered the clearing. The cool, calm night made it easy to see the moon, which sat high in the sky, fat and full. As he approached, his best friend, Travon, tossed him a beer from the cooler. It was Tray's own microbrew and some of the best he had ever had. He took a long, satisfying drink and stood in front of the fire, watching it dance. He met eyes with Mathias and Nathaniel across the huge blaze and began walking over to them.

The three had been his best friends since their days in detention. It was hard to be a young black man in the world. Every grumble, frustration, or action was scrutinized, inflated, and then punished. They had met at Central High School in 2004 and had the distinction of being the last graduating class before the school closed. They had formed a bond when each of them ended up in detention every month around the same time. Gregory hugged each of them with a hard slap on the back.

The tension that sat in the air was palpable and made the small crowd animated in their conversations. About two dozen people milled about—drinking, laughing, and having a good time around the fire. The rowdiness calmed suddenly, and he looked up.

"It is that joyous time that we get to embrace our nature and live freely. Once upon a time, it was thought of as a curse, but we know better. We are children of the moon, and each month we are allowed to break free of our human shells, embrace our instinct, and become one with our natural surroundings."

Gregory lifted his bottle and cheered with the others at the arrival of their leader, Marcus. The tall, dark-skinned man stood on the far side of the fire from him. His smile reflected the firelight, but his warm, brown eyes met with every single member there. He had been the visiting social worker at Central High School. More importantly he had saved each and every one of them from a future in a cell. Better yet, he helped them to make sense of what had been going on, but he also forced them to excel so that they could not only survive but prosper. The boys owed not just their freedom, but their sanity to him. Loyalty had been earned with each counseling session, group meeting, and the night he saved them from tearing out each other's throats.

They had learned they were lost werewolf cubs and that their race had mixed with humans long ago to help perpetuate survival. Over the years, especially in the Dark Ages, they became prey for the local, religious leaders to help set examples of Satan's wickedness. Their people fled for their lives and went into hiding. So sometimes, a shifter was born without knowing what he was. Marcus's family had decided that their job was to find the lost cubs and bring them into their fold. In the past, they had gone through the insane asylums and jails. Currently, they looked for kids in juvenile detention centers. Marcus had taken it one step further and tried to find them before they got in the system.

"Let us go. We hunt for our feast, we hunt to embraces ourselves, and we hunt to further our bond as a pack!"

There were hearty cheers and clinking of bottles. The pack disrobed quickly as the tug of the moon compelled them to change into their lupine forms. Gregory stretched and stood comfortably naked as he waited for the change to take him. His neck popped, and he relaxed and let nature take its course. He leaned over as his bones shifted and became better suited for running on all four legs instead of two. His soft under fur grew in, even as a coarse coat covered it. As his body finished, his eyes changed and the night around him burst into life. One of the things he loved most about being a wolf was the night vision. He could see a chipmunk scurry through the trees around them and watched the bats as they hunted for insects in the air.

Marcus raised his snout and loosed a deep, reverberating howl into the air. The pack followed suit. As the wolf-song died out, the hunt started. Despite the law of men saying that deer hunting started in November, the pack hunted each month. It not only kept the local herd culled to a reasonable—fewer than car accidents—level. It also reminded them to work and celebrate as a pack.

Gregory scented a doe, and giving a nod to his friends, they stretched out and planned to run her down and then turn her back to the pack. He followed Mathias, who nipped at her ankles. She was older, probably had given birth twice, but still spry and gave them a good chase. Gregory took in a deep breath of crisp air and lowered himself closer to the ground as he prepared to put on a burst of speed. His heart thudded in his chest as adrenaline filled his system; his paws pressed flat and propelled him towards the doe. The scent of fear made his mouth water. He turned her back towards his pack, baying his success. Dark shapes flanked him, and he grinned as his friends joined him and moved the deer forward. A sleek, tawny, lupine shape flew by them in a ground-eating pace and launched at the deer's neck. It was down and still in mere moments.

Gregory shifted back with a grin of triumph. He loved hunting.

"We will eat well tonight," he said.

The group around him also reverted to their man forms.

"You always did have a good knack for turning them back," Mathias said, looking at the doe.

The tawny colored wolf trotted over to the group, shifted back, and smiled.

"Good work, guys. Gregory, will you carry her back?"

"Sure thing, Tess. Nice kill," Gregory said as he slung the doe over his shoulders.

He couldn't wait for the real party to start.

Chapter 5

Flora stood in front of her mirror and switched her outfits back and forth. She had errands to run and, with the temperatures expecting to reach the high nineties, she needed to look professional but also be prepared for the heat. As a marketing ploy, she did a lot of networking and selling when she did her errands, so she dressed for it. She knew she was her brand and identity, so she had made the decision not to walk out of her house dressed for anything less than a business encounter, ever.

So far, it had netted one client, but she considered it a good start. Flora knew times were tough and selling her services would be hard. Factory towns had an interesting dichotomy. People were used to working hard to earn their keep, and that was great. The flip side was that they were slow to change, and while they understood the internet was a thing, using programs for marketing or inventory seemed foreign and odd to them.

Finally, she settled on the lime-green sundress, because she had a matching hat. As she slid her feet into her chunky heeled Mary Jane's, she was finally ready to go. Flora figured she could get all of her errands done before her noon dance class and then hopefully spend the rest of the day figuring out how to make her database project move quickly. To her delight, her morning went exactly as planned. She had gotten a full half of her errands done, handed out business cards to some local businesses, and overall managed not to sweat profusely. She had just finished grabbing mail from her post office box when she turned and bumped into another person.

"I am so sorry. I wasn't paying any sort of…"

Her voice trailed off as her eyes rose up to meet Gregory's. The amused twinkle in his eyes made her blush. After the very erotic foot massage a few days before, she had not seen him at the park. Not for lack of trying on her part.

"Gregory," she breathed his name.

"Good morning, Flora," he said. "This is a pleasant surprise."

She smiled, and it grew wider and more awkward as words failed her. Flora's mind spun as she tried to figure out what to talk to him about.

"So, they do let you out of the park," she said.

Flora immediately regretted that her mind hadn't figured out something less stupid to say to him.

"Periodically," he chuckled. "But only when I promise to be on my best behavior."

Her hot face meant the blush had deepened, and Flora dropped her gaze.

"Right, that was silly of me to say," she said. "Let's try this again. How is your morning, Gregory?"

"Better now," he said. "I had a great session with the kids on the Turtlemobile, and I got to see you. How is your day?"

"I'm just out running errands," she said. "Just a regular day in my life."

Flora shifted slightly from foot to foot as he nodded and smiled at her. She was frustrated that she couldn't think of how to interact with him. He had only given her a foot rub; it wasn't as if they had slept together. She had no idea why he made her so flustered. And then in her moment of unease, she did the stupidest thing possible. She opened her mouth.

"I don't suppose you are free to run errands and keep me company? I'll treat you to lunch afterwards."

The words slid over her tongue and out of her mouth before she knew it. His brow arched and then a heart-stopping smile covered his face. He held up a pile of brochures.

"That sounds great. Let me finish up here, and I will be ready to join you."

While Gregory stood in line to mail out his brochures Flora nervously paced.

"What did I just do?" she muttered to herself. "Holy crap, I just invited him to walk around town with me. Why does he even think running errands sounds like fun? Please let today be the day where everyone I know is busy."

She paced a bit more as the line in the post office seemed to move slowly. Flora had to turn in an invoice to the Flint Public Library, and pick up some dry cleaning.

"Sure, Gregory, come on along and watch my oh-so-boring life."

She was glad he stood at the counter chatting away with the Post Master. She absolutely wanted to spend time with him, but asking him to walk around and pretty much do nothing else seemed to be a stupid idea.

"At least I was smart enough to ask him to lunch," she said. "But where do I take him? I don't even know what he likes to eat."

She managed to stop talking to herself as Gregory approached her. She smiled sincerely as he got close.

"Well, I hope you know what you just got yourself into," she said.

"Unless you plan to drag me off to some Ladies Auxiliary meeting for hours, I think I will be fine with your errands," he teased back.

"Well, I was thinking you might be squeamish getting a mani and pedi with me."

Flora schooled her face to remain serene as his eyes searched for a hint of teasing or truth. She watched his mouth quirk, making his dimple appear.

"I usually get those on Sunday, but I can rearrange my schedule."

She picked up his hand and ran her fingers over the calluses on his palm. She then turned his hand over and examined his fingers.

"You should get a better girl. It looks like she has no idea how to trim back your cuticles properly."

Flora smiled widely as he adjusted their hands so that he could grip hers. He gave her fingers a quick examination and looked at her.

"Your girl has it easy, though," he said.

"How so?" Flora questioned.

"Well, naturally, you already have soft and perfect hands. How much work does she actually have to do on you? My hands are all rough and manly, not delicate like yours. There is absolutely no hope of my ever having soft hands. It doesn't matter how excellent she is.

Flora snorted, yet allowed him to continue to hold her hand.

"Like you have ever had a mani in your life."

"I sure have," he said.

"Riiight. There is a better chance of me going hiking in the woods with you than you ever having had a manicure in your life."

"Is that a challenge, Flora Blu?" he asked.

"Whatever you want to make of it, Gregory," she laughed. "Okay, I have two errands to do before we have lunch. I think it best that we get my dry cleaning and then go to the library. That way, we will be closer to downtown and all the restaurants."

"Lead the way," he said.

They had easy conversation as they walked to her car and drove to the dry cleaner. Fate had even smiled up on her, and Flora found street parking only a few feet away from the shop. Regrettably, Gregory had had to let her hand go so that she could drive, and Flora didn't have enough nerve to grab his and hold it again as they walked towards the building.

"And that was how I ended up on the homecoming court junior year and fulfilled my five-year-old self's fantasy of being a princess," she finished. "I even got to wear a tiara."

Flora smiled as Gregory held the door for her and started to walk, but she stopped short in the entryway.

An icy pit formed in her stomach, and her heart started hammering. She felt him bump into her as she ceased all movement. Her brain spun furiously to think of an excuse to get them out of there as quickly as possible with minimal fuss. Flora knew she had to pretend to be calm. Otherwise, it might lead to a conversation which could keep them there longer. And then it would get worse. She took a breath, and thankfully, her brain kicked back in and gave her the perfect excuse.

"Oh damn, Gregory. I totally forgot that Eileen at the library said she had to leave before lunch. I need to go grab that invoice from her," she said, impressed that her voice sounded calm to her own ears.

Flora had already turned around and grabbed his hand as she led him out of the store. She wanted to tug and pull him along faster, but instead forced herself to take normal steps.

"Okay, Flora," he said calmly. "Don't worry. I am sure we will get there in time."

"I just hate leaving my clients waiting," she said. "I am my brand, so every action I make reflects my business."

Flora managed not to gun the engine as she pulled away from the dry cleaning store. She even made sure that she kept to the speed limit. It wasn't until the car was two stoplights away from the dry cleaner that she was able to breathe.

Okay, breathe and act calm. We dodged a horrible situation. I do not think she saw us, so we are okay. In what convoluted universe does my mother pick up her dry cleaning at eleven on Wednesdays? She is supposed to be at the church for the church school meetings! Or women's ministry meeting or something, but not picking up clothes. I cannot even imagine what kind of disaster would have happened if she would have seen me with Gregory. I mean, it looks like we are together, but heck, this lunch with him is anything that comes close to us having a first date. I am so not ready to explain to her who he is and why I am with him. We made it to the library and my phone has not rung, so we are in the clear. Stay calm. It's not as if I want to have to explain that to him.

"We're here," she announced a bit too brightly. "Let's go get that invoice."

It ended up being a much quicker trip than she had expected. Somehow, her excuse had morphed into reality and Eileen had already left for the day to attend a meeting. However, the invoice was waiting for her at the front desk. She didn't actually know any of the librarians enough to engage in small talk. So they were in and out in less than five minutes. Flora worried briefly that her mother would still be at the dry cleaner, but her luck held out and no one was in the store when they returned. She made the usual small talk but kept the visit short. After she put her clothes in her car, she looked at Gregory.

"Okay, all the boring errands are done. Isn't my life exciting? The good news is that I'm free for the rest of the day. Are you ready for some lunch?"

"Sure," he said and grinned at her. "You're like a little whirlwind. I think am exhausted just watching you run these two errands. I might just need a nap if we spend the whole day together."

"Nap? I can't remember the last time I took a nap. Anyhow, do you like barbeque?"

"Who doesn't love a good brisket?" Gregory replied.

Flora took him to her favorite smokehouse and almost sighed in quiet relief when they were put in a fairly private back corner. There was only one other seated table, so the area was quiet. They quickly ordered their food and resumed chatting. So far, Flora had told him about her adventures in being on the homecoming court as well as her one study-abroad semester in India. She had learned about his degree in testudinology and the outreach work he did with his mentor.

"I hope you don't mind if I say grace," she said as their food arrived.

"Please do," he said.

Flora was pleased to see him respectfully bow his head as she said a short blessing over the food. They then resumed eating their lunch and having light conversation. She was mid-laugh when movement caught her eye. She turned to get a better look and froze in place.

Oh, no, no, no…

"Sister Blu, so good to see you."

"Pastor Jennings, how very nice to see you as well," Flora said, standing to receive his hug.

"I wanted to wait until your lunch was completed before I came over to greet you. I was just pleased to see you saying grace before your meal. So many people are afraid to bow their heads. It warmed my heart to see you living your faith out loud."

"Thank you, Pastor," she said.

Flora smiled and sat back down, figuring that the pastor wouldn't want to be rude and would quickly move on. He didn't.

"Hello, I am Pastor Jennings. I don't believe we have had the pleasure of meeting before."

"Gregory Bell. Nice to meet you."

Flora wanted to shrink and scurry away as Gregory stood and shook hands with her pastor.

And to think I was worried that my mom would see him. Well played, God.

"I certainly hope to see you joining Sister Blu at one of our services soon," Pastor Jennings said and then turned to leave. "Have a blessed day."

Flora watched him walk away and then turned to see Gregory giving her a knowing smile.

"Well, that couldn't have been comfortable," he said.

"It was awkward," she admitted. "But no worries. He is a very nice man."
She smiled and tried to get back to the place of easy conversation with

Gregory. She found that it was harder to get back into that space. As she was grasping for something to talk about, her phone chimed with a text message.

"Do you feel up to one more errand?"

"Sure. Where are we off to now?"

"The print shop. I'm going to be at the Women's Expo this year, so I ordered a huge banner," she said. "They just texted me to let me know it's in. It's only a few blocks away. I figure it would be silly for me not to grab it while I am here."

She let Gregory hold her chair as she stood and then felt a warm tingle in the pit of her stomach as he held her hand again. Part of her was tempted to look around for her pastor, but she didn't want Gregory to think that she was jumpy or ashamed to be seen with him. Not to mention, she really did enjoy holding his hand.

As they walked down the street, she noticed that his steps began to slow. She looked around and then grinned at him.

"Why are we stopping at a nail shop?"

"Well, you said you would go hiking with me if I had ever had a manicure."

"Nuh uh. This won't count, Gregory. You can't get one now just to try to win."

"Ah, Flora Blu, I don't plan to get one now. I just want to introduce you to the nail tech that gave me my mani," he said as a lazy smile covered his face. "Because I really want to see you hiking."

"I don't recall my making it a challenge," she said, desperately trying to backpedal.

"Actually, you allowed me to decide whether or not it was going to be a challenge," he said. "And I figured, why not?"

"Well…"

"Are you going to chicken out?"

"I'm not afraid of a little hike," she countered. "I just didn't agree to your terms."

"Too late to back out, Flora Blu," he said as he opened the door. "I am going to plan the best hike ever. Three days from now, prepare to see For-Mar a whole new way. Now, come in and meet Monica."

Flora swallowed a sigh and paused at the door. She hated the idea of failing.

"Fine."

She walked into the shop with a smile on her face and met Gregory's nail tech, who corroborated the story. She gave him a look letting him know how she felt about being set up. He chuckled at her. On the one hand, she would be spending more time with Gregory. But it would be outdoors, with all the nature. She wasn't quite sure she would survive it.

Chapter 6

"Thanks for meeting with me, Tess and Gregory," Marcus said. "Come in and have a seat. I have been very busy and haven't had time to really address the issues we need to cover.

Gregory felt like a schoolboy called into the principal's office. He walked into the small room and then gestured for Tess to sit first. Taking a deep breath, he sat next to her and tried to project calm. He had known they would be having this meeting soon, but he wasn't prepared for the rush of nervousness that coursed through his veins. All of a sudden, everything got real, with major changes and huge consequences.

"I know there has been a lot of speculation and rumors. I would like to end all the hearsay now."

Gregory felt that each word coming out of Marcus's mouth dripped in molasses-like slowness. He looked for a sign of anything on his mentor's face. Not a quirk of the lip or a blink gave anything away.

"Gregory, I have decided that, if you accept, you will start training to be the next Alpha," Marcus said after a slight pause. "Tess, you are a strong leader and a great Beta, and I know that you will help Gregory as he prepares for this new role. You are a great asset to the pack and maybe even someday you will become a leader."

"Thank you, Marcus, but you know that I am happy to be Beta. I never wanted to lead, just be a strong pack member and support."

"Well, it is appreciated. You are a highly regarded member of our group," Marcus said.

Gregory looked at Tess, who gave him a slight smile. He didn't quite understand her reasons for not wanting to be Alpha, but he was glad that Marcus picked him all the same. The rumors had been mostly true after all. The false part was that Tess would contest and all sorts of trouble would ensue.

"I think this will be good," Gregory said. "I am eager to learn from the best."

"Thanks, Gregory," Tess said.

He accepted the quick hug from her and rolled his eyes when she winked at him as she walked out of the office. A smile creased his face in relief and victory. He watched the door shut and then turned to face his Alpha. He held out his hand and met Marcus's halfway across the desk.

"I look forward to working with you," he said with a smile.

"Glad to hear that," Marcus said. "It will be hard work, but I have no doubt you are up to the challenge. Have a seat. There is a lot to prepare you for."

Gregory sat back down, glad to again be so closely tied to his mentor. He was certain there would be a lot of hard work. Marcus had created and maintained a pack that helped and supported each other, and it wouldn't be easy to fill such an important role. Through the years, he and Marcus had talked for hours about the direction the pack should go and how to help it grow and prosper.

Unlike the ideas shown by popular media, being a pack member was rather like having an exclusive membership, but each person had control over the amount of interaction they had. The Alpha was chosen by their predecessor, and there was no fight to the death. When a pack member wanted to leave, they were able. It didn't mean that fights and other craziness were absent; however, Marcus had had few major issues with his pack, and Gregory planned to continue the trend.

Gregory looked down at his watch again and found that a whole forty-two seconds had passed. He had spent two days trying to plan the perfect hike for Flora. He had picked an easy but beautiful route, only 8/10 of a mile. The path was in full bloom, and he was eager to show her. He had also packed a light lunch. As he looked at the basket, he realized he was actually nervous to go on this date. He had been pleased with his clever plan, but later as he tried to plan the event, he found himself mad that he couldn't just ask her out without a bet.

Before he could grumble about being too scared to ask her out, he saw her car pull into the lot. He unabashedly stared as Flora got out of her car and with a huge smile, began to walk towards him. Gregory was relieved to see that she wore tennis shoes.

"Hi, Flora," he greeted, pulling her into a hug.

"Good morning, Gregory," she said. "Let's go get this hike thing done."

"Awww, Sweetheart, you're breaking my heart. A hike is meant to be enjoyable. I picked a great path," he said and stepped back to show her the basket. "I even packed us a picnic"

He had to resist the urge to lean in and kiss her wrinkled nose.

"Come on. I survived meeting your pastor. I doubt we will have anything that exciting happen out here," he said.

Gregory laughed as Flora stared at him with hands on her hips. He grabbed the picnic basket by the handles and extended his left hand out to her. She paused, and he gave her what he hoped was a charming grin.

"Shall we?"

Gregory felt a warm rush from the smile Flora gave him in return.

"Absolutely."

The Lilac Walk was pretty isolated as they walked through. There were a variety of the blooming bushes, in various shades of purples and whites. The scent wafted through the air, and while Gregory didn't care one way or another for it, Flora inhaled deeply.

"I love lilacs," she said. "My grandparents used to have them all around their house. When I was a little girl and had sleepovers, my grandpa would always have a fresh bunch at the table for breakfast. My parents have bushes grown from the clippings and when I get my own house, I plan to have some too."

"What a great memory," he said. "I actually didn't know anything about them until I started working here. In my first week, I made the huge mistake of calling them a tree, and Ginny promptly schooled me on the differences in height and branch structure. Don't mess with that woman and her lilacs."

They laughed as they walked in a lazy pace along the path. At top speed, Gregory could make it around in just under ten minutes, but he wanted to draw out the time he had with Flora. The weather had decided to accommodate him, and even though it was warm, a light breeze kept it cool enough. He began to tell her about the rowdy group of boys who took on the challenge of climbing some of the taller bushes and about Ginny's reaction. He turned to face her when she stopped walking and found a look of sheer horror had crossed Flora's face as she stood still.

"Flora?"

"I think a bird just crapped on me, Gregory."

He gave her credit for not being completely hysterical, even though her voice sounded like she might just get there pretty fast. He stopped and looked her over, and indeed, there was a small, wet pile on her left shoulder. He quickly reached into the basket and pulled out a package of wipes.

"Let me help," he said.

He gently pressed one wipe under the shoulder of her shirt, glad it was sleeveless, and used the wipe on top of the shirt to remove the offending mess.

"One thing I learned in college is that you always try to remove a stain the way it landed. So, pressing up against the fabric should leave less of a mark."

Gregory knew he was rambling, but he had promised Flora a fun hike. Somehow he doubted that being crapped on by a bird would make her top ten fun memories. He had the mess cleaned up and quickly put the wipes in a plastic bag. He met her eyes and silently implored her to stay with him just a while longer. She took a deep breath and relaxed.

"Ready to move on?"

Flora nodded and didn't pull her hand away when he reached for hers again. After a few heavy seconds of bird chatter that highlighted the silence, she even talked to him again.

"Why would you have learned that in turtle college?"

"My roommate's mother was a seamstress, and he was a bit obsessed about different fabrics. Of course, it might have been from the time I came back from a bonfire and puked all over his bed," Gregory said with a grin. "My hangover the next day was made worse by the task of cleaning up my own mess. Not only did he stand over me until I was awake, I had to take care of it immediately, and he was insistent that I do it the proper way. So, as I blotted away, I got a lecture on the history and proper care of comforters and duvet covers. I also know why cotton is the preferred material."

"Wow, a man who knows what a duvet is," she teased.

"Hey, now, there are plenty of guys who know what a duvet cover is," he scolded her.

"True enough. However, most of them like each other."

"I detect a bit of sexism here," Gregory laughed.

"No," she corrected. "For as many friends as I have, the only guy I know—aside from you—who knows what a duvet cover is is definitely gay."

Gregory nodded. As they came to the bend in the path, he veered off and led her behind the bushes. When she gave him a questioning look, he grinned.

"The advantage of working here is that I won't get fined for having a picnic here."

"Aren't you setting a bad example?" Flora asked with an arched eyebrow.

"Of course not. Do you think I would be crazy enough to cross Ginny by trampling her lilacs? Although, if the bushes get hurt, I will blame your stunning brown eyes for any lapse in judgement."

He loved the way her body went into her laugh; her eyes widened and then her mouth crinckled at the sides. As the sound worked its way up from her belly, her shoulders pulled back in an undulating ripple and moved with her in her mirth.

"Well, if one glimpse of my eyes makes you lose yourself, I'm afraid of what could happen if perhaps you saw any more skin."

The words caught him unprepared, and Gregory felt his heart leap as Flora gave him a sassy wink. He spread a blanket and then pulled out a few containers with various fruits, cheese, and crackers. An easy conversation flowed between the two of them as they enjoyed their snack. Gregory took a chance, and after he fed a particularly fat and juicy strawberry to Flora, he kissed her. She tasted of berries and sweetness. To his delight, she returned his affections eagerly. With some restraint, he ended their embrace and went back to feeding her various fruits. He held up a nice black fruit, and her nose wrinkle came back.

"You don't like mulberries?" he asked.

"I don't even know what one is," Flora said.

"Then try one," Gregory said with a short laugh. "They are delicious."

He nuzzled the berry against her lips until she finally took a nibble. She stared at him a moment and then nipped at his fingers before she finished the offering. She accepted the second and third with a laugh.

"Yes, they are good," she said. "The second best thing I have had on my lips today."

Gregory took the not too subtle hint and kissed her. He savored each gentle sweep of her tongue as the slow and gentle touches tasted of her. Animated toddler squeals and chatter broke the sensual haze, and they smiled at each other. With a shrug, he began to pack up the remnants of their picnic and put them in the basket.

"Ready to finish the hike?"

"Sure," Flora said as she helped him clean the area. She held the basket by the handles and walked back toward the path. "You know, this wasn't—"

The high-pitched alarm that emitted from her mouth had him on his feet and at her side before he knew what was wrong. As Gregory watched, she began swiping at her face in frantic movements. He wondered if she had gotten stung by a bee or a wasp.

"Flora, what happened?" he asked. "Are you okay?"

"It's all over meeeee," she wailed. "A spider web!"

He grabbed a tissue and ran it over her face in a counter-clockwise motion. Gregory wiped her face one more time. She started to calm down and stared at him with wide eyes.

"There, it's all gone," he said in a soothing voice.

He pulled her close and enveloped her in a hug. He could feel Flora tremble and felt bad for her scare. He couldn't actually see the web that she had walked into, so he hoped he could convince her to finish their walk.

"All better? Okay, we're near the end, so let's leave."

"Why are there so many bugs everywhere?" she asked. "There is no need for spiders to be here in the lilac bushes."

Gregory wisely held his tongue as he picked up the basket. He then held his hand out to her. He nodded at the young mother, who looked at them with concern. "Spiderwebs," he mouthed, and she smiled. They walked around the rest of the path. He smiled as she began to relax again while he told her about his less than illustrious sports career in high school. Despite being fairly tall and well built, basketball had been a disaster.

"Yeah, there were points where I watched the coach just shake his head in amazed disappointment with me," he said with a grin. "Baseball was just an exercise in swing and miss."

He didn't mind that she giggled at him. Gregory hadn't been sure the date could be salvaged after the spiderweb thing, but now she was relaxed and listening to him with rapt attention. He carefully built up the momentum as he told her about his different sports-related trials. They had made it to the end of the walk, and he smiled.

"You made it," he said. "You survived the nature walk."

"It wasn't even a mile, Gregory," she said. "I'm not that out of shape."

"I like your shape just fine," he said. He didn't bother to point out her adverse reactions to the nature around her versus the physical workout. "Let's go check on those turtles before we leave. Besides, I have one more sport to cover."

Gregory smiled at Flora and launched into his days as a football player.

"I was pretty solid and I didn't fall down when others ran into me," he said. "So it was the one sport where I actually did something right. Block others."

They laughed as they walked down the small hill and around to the back of the pond. He stood amazed as Flora explained how she hoped to not only create a database but also get some amazing shots for the center. The turtles must have sensed her excitement because they came out to show interest. Gregory held her hand as she leaned out over the pond, trying to catch a shot of the stack of turtles sunning on the far log, when a telltale gust of wind blew past them. He raised his eyes just in time to see fat drop of water dropping from the sky. He pulled Flora in quickly.

Really, Nature? You already threw enough at her. This was supposed to be a good date. Do you really hate her as much as she hates you?

The rain moved from thick drops into a sheet of liquid faster than he had ever seen. As they slogged their way back around the pond, the ground grew muddy and slick. Nothing was said as they made their way up the hill. They stood at the top of the hill, and Gregory looked at the visitor's center.

"I think I am ready to go home," Flora said.

He stared at her wide eyes that threatened tears and noted the firm press of her lips. He wanted to tell her that she had been brave, but he figured that might be her tipping point and he let it rest. They walked to her car in silence. Gregory found himself impressed as she pulled a plastic tarp from the back and covered her seat before sitting. He wondered why she had the tarp but didn't ask. He leaned in to kiss her and was glad when she met him halfway.

"Thank you for taking a walk with me," he said.

"It wasn't all bad," she said. "Next time, I get to choose our date venue. Something inside."

He nodded and watched as she drove away. At least she had said 'next time.'

Chapter 7

"Flora!"

Flora startled out of her musings and looked at the smiling eyes of her friend. The raised eyebrow and tilted head did not detract from her otherwise beautiful friend.

"Yes? I'm listening," she said and speared a piece of grilled asparagus with her fork.

She saw the quirk of Shonise's lips and realized not only had she been caught with her head in the clouds, but she also really must have been in her own world for quite a while. She tried to replay the last few sentences she had heard but realized the last thing she remembered was ordering her dinner.

"Really? Because I just suggested that we rent a cabin and rough it for a week, and you agreed," Shonise said. "You know, the rustic cabins. Down in Brighton."

"I did no such thing," Flora said, trying her best to control her face from looking horrified. She made a show of deliberately eating three spears of asparagus with exaggerated slowness. "We both know that anything with the title 'rustic' means no indoor plumbing. You would rather go out bare-faced to the store than stay in anything rustic. What's up, needy one?

The blatant stare giving her serious shade gave her no warning for the next question.

"Who is he?"

Her eyes snapped up from her plate to her friend's face. For about ten seconds, Flora contemplated lying. Then Shonise winked at her, and she knew there was no reason to even try. She was already caught. They had been best friends since they were five years old. They had met the first day of kindergarten where they had fought over the computer during free period. Shonise had won that time, and they had been best friends ever since.

"Just a park ranger who helped me out of a pond," Flora said.

She neglected telling Shonise about the impromptu dates just yet.

"A park ranger?" Shonise started to ask.

Flora waved her fork dismissively and tried to go back to her grilled ahi.

"I can't understand how you talked me into this…stuff," she grumbled. "I really don't like fish."

"But this is ahi tuna from Hawaii," Shonise smiled. "You have to expand your menu."

"What is wrong with some good ole', Midwestern beef? We have a lot of cows that are waiting to be on the grill."

"Nice try, but that won't work. Now, spill," Shonise said.

"Why do you even ask?"

"Because you are all lit up like a Christmas tree. Now, who is he?"

"He works at For-Mar. And after he saved me from being eaten alive by their carnivorous fish, he gave me a foot massage to help me relax," Flora said and, giving up, waved over the waitress. "I need a rare T-bone please. I can't eat this."

"For-Mar has carnivorous fish?"

"Piranhas, I'm pretty sure. Because when I stepped in the pond, they tried to eat me. That's why Gregory had to give me a foot massage."

"Piranhas are native to the Amazon basin. They are not in Michigan."

"Right, like people don't sneak exotic pets into the country all the damn time. Like anacondas are native to the Everglades," Flora said.

"Stop stalling. So, was this massage from Gregory with your clothes on?" Shonise asked.

"Of course. How could you ask such a thing?"

"Because you are glowing. GLOW-ing," her friend said with a smirk. "It must have been one heck of a massage. Are you sure it was only on your feet?"

Flora couldn't help the blush that raced up her neck and over her cheeks. Remembering Gregory's firm touch made her smile. It had been an amazing experience, but even that had paled compared to the kiss he had given her in the rain. The knowing grin on Shonise's face made her reign in the lustful thoughts.

"It most definitely was fully dressed. Now, stop saying things like that before someone overhears and my Mama hears the gossip," she said, shaking her head. "He's just a nice guy that works there."

"Huh," Shonise snorted. "Girl, are you listening to you? First, you tell me he is a park ranger, and then he gave you a massage after you stepped in water with fish. You, Flora Blu, abhor nature. There has got to be a lot more to this story."

Flora sighed happily as a nice, rare steak was set before her and made her bestie wait a full three forkfuls of satin beef heaven before answering her.

"For-Mar hired me to create a database of their box turtles. I figured they would be in a display like at a zoo or something, but no, they are out in a pond. I was setting up my cameras to catch pictures of their shells when I felt something try to strip the flesh from my bones. Gregory was there to catch me before I fell in the water. Then he gave me the most glorious foot massage I have ever had," Flora rushed out.

She went back to eating her steak, despite the impatient look from her friend. She smiled sweetly as she took a sip of wine and sat back contented.

"That's all?"

"Well, we did have two impromptu dates," Flora said. "I asked him out to lunch, where we ran into Pastor Jennings."

"How could you keep this from me?" Shonise squealed. "Flora, you better not turn into one of those women who doesn't talk to their friends because a man is in their life."

"Honestly, Shonise, this has all been so fast, I don't know what to make of it all."

"You could make a lot more sense with two of us figuring it out. You held out on me for three dates," Shonise grumped.

Flora realized her friend was correct and quickly filled her in on the hiking date, fully appreciating the noises of sympathy that her friend made. She was even able to laugh a bit about being in the rain, and Shonise joined her.

"When are you going to offer to cook for him?" Shonise asked.

"Soon," she laughed. "I figure I owe him a debt for his kindness. Not to mention, he is seriously gorgeous."

The women ordered another bottle of wine to go with their decadent cheesecake and put their heads together to plan the perfect dinner. Flora's tablet sat between them on the table as they created a musical and mood lighting scheme to go with the food and drinks.

Early the next morning, Flora—armed with galoshes, rubber gloves that fit up to her elbow, and a mosquito hat—strode toward the pond with the intention of getting her equipment set up. She was ready to be done with the nature part of the project.

"I do not understand why these turtles are not on display," she muttered again to herself. "I get that people want to experience nature, but sometimes it is just easier to look at them in a nice glass display."

She waded in the pond and to her dismay found every single monopod had shifted. After calculating a few angles, she spent an extra seventy-five minutes adjusting and pushing the sticks further into the pond bottom. Once secure, she placed the camera, safely encased in the waterproof case, on the mount. She checked and double checked to make sure that everything was stable before pushing the whole contraption back down under the water. She held her breath and when no bubbles rose the surface, smiled. She pulled out her tablet and hoped that the Bluetooth devices would easily pair up. Flora grimaced as the 'wheel of death' spun for a full two minutes.

"We are not going to do this every time I want to come out here and get pictures. The whole point of having shortwave radio transmissions is to make life easier," she lectured her tablet.

Finally, the devices paired, and Flora took a few test shots. She knew the waterproof case might make for some blurriness in the pictures, but she hoped to get enough clear shots. To her delight, the pictures were good and showed a decent amount of detail.

Flora took her time making sure each new camera was in a slightly different position to cover all the angels as she set them. She saw a fish or two but didn't bother to stomp at them since they had yet to sink their teeth past the rubber of her boots. She idly hoped that the camera would also catch the fish in the action of mauling something so she would have picture proof to show Shonise. She had taken a good amount of eye-rolling and condescending pats on the shoulder after having told her story.

"This is why people eat you," she snarled down at the fish. "No one likes to be nibbled on. For real, you should be smarter than to pick on something so far up the food chain from you. You're lucky I didn't bring a spear to defend myself."

Two hours later, Flora had completed setting up her cameras and checking them. She had even been lucky enough to snap several pictures of turtles while doing test shots. There had been quite a few of them that wanted to pose for the camera, and she was delighted because it gave her some primary identifiers to work with as she set up her program. She figured that she would need to come back at least every other day and download the information off of the cameras, but she knew within a couple of days she would have enough to get the database started.

Flora walked back to her car slowly. She knew she dragged her feet so she could possibly run into Gregory. As she walked past the center, she decided to avoid going in because of the squirming, wriggling masses of children. Even if he was in there, he would be working, and she knew better than to try to interrupt someone at their job. She walked to her car, pulled off the galoshes, and put on her comfortable, strappy sandals. She took a deep breath; it was already hot at ten thirty in the morning.

"You got some jokes, Michigan," she muttered.

Flora looked up in time to see a crowd of kids leave the center, but she couldn't see who the leader was. She sighed and trudged back to the center. Ginny was there, with her ever present, bright smile, and much to Flora's annoyance, she looked refreshed.

"Hey, Ginny. Is Gregory around?" she asked, forcing her voice to be light and friendly.

"Sorry, Flora, you just missed him. He just took that energetic bunch of teens out for a two-hour tour."

Flora couldn't imagine a worse sounding activity in her life.

"Does he have a mailbox or something so I can leave him a note? He offered to help me set up, but we missed each other," she said. "I need to let him know not to touch anything."

Ginny chuckled and handed her a notebook.

"You don't want him in there messing up all of your hard work?"

"Pretty much," Flora said with a grin.

She scrawled a mundane letter to him and left her phone number. Then she added a smiley face and a threat of bodily harm if he touched her equipment. She grinned at Ginny, thanked her, and walked back out to her car.

Flora went back to her office and sat staring at her screen. She knew that Gregory wouldn't even read her note until the afternoon, but she was still anxious. Instead of pacing like a caged creature at home, she opted to go for a double workout. She took a refreshing shower, and as she stood in front of her closet pondering what to wear, her phone rang again. She grabbed her Bluetooth headset and clicked it on.

"Flora Blu Designs," she said automatically as she pulled a lavender skirt from her closet.

"Is this the same Flora Blu who threatened me great bodily harm if I touched her equipment?"

The rich, melted chocolate of Gregory's voice slid over her and goosebumps rose on her arms at the innuendo lacing his words.

"Were you naughty, Gregory?" she asked, deliberately lowering her voice.

No way was she backing down from this game. She grinned as he chuckled into the phone, and she became aware exactly how little she wore as they talked. Even though he couldn't see her, she reached out and grabbed a sleeveless, white, mock t-neck and held it next to the skirt.

"What if I were?"

She raised an eyebrow at herself in the mirror.

"Well then, you certainly would not receive the offer of my making dinner for you tonight."

"Then it is a good thing I didn't touch anything, especially your equipment," he said quickly.

She laughed, and he joined her.

"Smart man. How was the tour? Have you recovered?"

"The tour was filled with twenty teenagers who would have rather spent all day looking at their phones; so, lots of whining," he said. "I am sure I will have recovered by tonight. By the way, I apologize for not helping you this morning. One of our guides called in sick, and I had to sub."

"No worries," she said. "I got them all set up and synced. And you will be pleased to know that no fish attacked me today."

He laughed again, and she smiled.

"What are you doing now?"

"Standing here, mostly naked, talking to you."

She could just imagine him swallowing against a dry throat at her statement. She managed not to giggle into the phone as the silence drew out. She looked at the time and dressed quickly.

"Well, not naked anymore. I have a meeting soon, and I just got dressed," she said airily. "Will seven this evening work for you?"

"Seven?" he asked.

"For dinner?" she asked.

"Right. Yes, seven o'clock sounds fine. What can I bring?" he asked.

"Whatever you want. I need to run. I will text you my address. See you tonight, Gregory."

She hung up after his goodbye and grabbed her business case. She smiled as she walked down the stairs. She had a dinner date and a new job. Her day was pretty damn perfect.

"Shonise," she said as she sat waiting for the car to cool down again. "Meet me at the Farmer's Market at four. I am cooking for Gregory tonight."

Chapter 8

Gregory shook his head as he hung up the phone. Flora Blu was a sassy tease, but she had invited him over for dinner. He looked toward the sky, the moon easily visible during the day. It was the last night of the full moon, and he would need to run. He decided that he wouldn't hunt with his pack, and realized that it would be the first one he had missed in years. However, there were no rules about having to run with the pack. It was offered, but he knew a few of the guys that preferred to run alone. Given what was going on, Gregory considered it might be just the right time to get really in touch with himself and run solo for a while. He smiled as he recalled the conversation with Flora. Once he saw her note, he knew he couldn't just let it go. And he even thought he had the upper hand with his intentionally sexual innuendo. Then she said she was nearly naked. Images had flooded his mind and rendered him unable to speak until she chided him.

She kept him off balance, and he liked it. She was smart as hell and opinionated but also uncertain when it came to being at the pond. He thought she was innovative to get pictures of the turtles instead of trying to trap them all. When he heard about the program, he had feared that some tiny, geeky dude would come in and try to set up traps and observe the turtles in a tank. He was much happier with who had shown up. Even though she had no idea how to dress for the job. Who came to a nature preserve in a high-heeled shoes? He hoped she had listened to him and bought a pair of galoshes that morning. Although, seeing her in that skirt was enough to make him think very naughty things about her.

"Damn good thing I am alone on this trail," he muttered to himself, putting himself in check before a tent rose.

Then again, he never would have called her with kids around. He refused to let them use their phones and refused to be a hypocrite with them. He walked down to the turtle pond and peered at all of the sticks in the water. Gregory chuckled as he imagined her trying to set it up, all the while keeping an eye out for the fish. He was impressed with she had gotten the cameras stabilized and quite frankly wanted to know how accurate his own cataloguing efforts had been. At last check, he had captured sixty different turtles. His watch beeped at him, reminding him that his next group was only thirty minutes away. He jogged up to the center to grab his lunch and relax before his next outing.

His phone buzzed two times as he sat eating lunch, but he forced himself not to answer. Seeing her texts would just make the afternoon go that much slower. Especially if she had decided to carry on the flirting session. He would just have to wait.

Gregory groaned as he stripped out of his uniform, dropped it on the floor, and headed to the shower. It had been a very hot seven miles around the reserve. The kids were high energy and fun, but even with frequent water breaks, the heat wore them down. Then, as he tried to leave, a very young and bubbly couple came to look at the arboretum. He had shown them to the area and stayed to answer the millions of questions. They were excited and took a ton of pictures to show the world where their wedding would be. He had gently reminded them to show up the next day to fill out paperwork so they could reserve it. Before he had actually made it to his bike, he was stopped again. The park didn't close until eight that night and random people were still on the trails

Normally, he didn't care, but he had dinner plans and needed to leave. He gave quick directions and then rode away as fast as possible.

He could admit it, he was excited that Flora was going to cook him dinner. He honestly didn't know what to expect but hoped that the food would be as good as the company. He enjoyed the time he spent with her, as little as it had been. She made him laugh a lot. She also had been seductively posing in his mind all afternoon, and he was more than ready to kiss her again. He stepped out of the shower and wrapped a towel around his waist. He sighed as he realized he hadn't thought about what to bring. It really did need to be good.

He supposed he could go with the bottle of wine route. It seemed safe. But Gregory didn't want to be safe. He wanted to continue the flirtation and see where it might take them. He thought about grabbing some wildflowers from the edge of his property, which sounded like a great idea, until he realized he had no idea if she had allergies. He could go for chocolates, but she might be high maintenance about her looks and look at it like it was poison.

"Back to wine," he shrugged as he pulled on a clean t-shirt and khaki shorts. "Face it, man, it has been so long since we have had a date, we don't even know what kind of gift to bring along anymore."

He checked his phone and true to her word, Flora had texted her address to him. The other messages had been from his friends about where to hang out after the run. He ignored those texts and went back to Flora's. He was almost a bit disappointed that she hadn't flirted with him via text. He started to reply with a sexy message three times before giving up. It would be easier to flirt in person. He was familiar with the area and knew a party store on the way. He shoved his feet into sandals, grabbed his keys, and walked out the door. He mentally tried to figure out what kind of wine he should bring her. Maybe just grab one of each to be safe? His thoughts stopped when he ran into someone. An amused smile met him as his guest gave his attire the once-over.

"I was just coming by to see what time you wanted to leave for the hunt," Tess said. "You're dressed kinda formal."

"Oh," Gregory said and then smiled. "I'm not gonna hunt tonight. I'll just go for a run later."

"Really? It's the last night," Tess said. "You haven't missed a hunt in years."

"I have other plans," he said. "Don't worry. I'll still shift and get my time in. I'll just be a lone wolf."

He tried to walk to his car, but Tess stepped into his path.

"Where are you going?"

"Tess," he said gently and gave her a smile. "I have other plans for tonight. Excuse me."

He couldn't miss the frown covering her face, but she moved. Gregory had absolutely no intention of explaining where he would be to her. Her being Beta only applied in pack matters. He waved to her as he got into his car and started it. He knew Tess was curious, but he was surprised at the scowl she gave him. When they had been together, she hadn't pried into his life. So why would she bother now? Even when she did find out that he had gone on a date, there was nothing she could do.

Enough of that. Let's focus on what will be happening tonight.

He bought wine on the way and in twenty minutes found himself standing outside her building. It was one of the newer, loft-style apartment buildings in Flint. The downtown area was revitalizing and slowly making the shift from a factory city to a college town, with some six or seven different universities, satellite campuses, and colleges in within a few square miles. He cleared his throat with a bit of jittery nerves and then rang her buzzer.

"Hello?" she asked.

"I come bearing gifts for one Ms. Flora Blu," he said.

"Come on in. I'm in apartment 402."

Gregory quickly climbed up the stairs and made it to her door. He had lifted his hand to knock when the door swung inward. Flora stood before him in a stunning, pale blue dress. He supposed she had a whole bunch of titles for the color, style, and fit, but he saw a desirable woman in a dress that gave more than a hint at the roundness of her breasts, hugged her waist, and swirled gently when she walked, showing her thighs.

"Come on in," she said with a welcoming gesture.

He walked in and was tempted by the smell of grilled filet mignon. His stomach rumbled and agreed that it was dinner time. Her apartment was cozy in decoration, with soft lights and instrumental music playing. It had a nice, open floorplan that included the kitchen, dining, and living rooms, with a staircase in view that he figured led up to the bedrooms.

"I brought wine," he said. "I wasn't sure what kind you liked, so I brought a random sampling."

She giggled at him, and he smiled back. He found her enticing and wanted to sweep her up into a kiss, but he could wait. He really did need some dinner, not to mention any forward actions would have been rude. Sure they had kissed before, but he didn't know if would be bad, since they were in the 'getting to know you' category. Gregory followed her into the kitchen and set the bottle on the counter. She then led him to the living room and to the couch.

"Can I offer you some of that wine?" she offered. "Thanks for bringing it."

"Sure. The rose should be still chilled enough," he said, sitting back.

He noticed as the music changed, the lighting made subtle changes as well. Flora came back and sat next to him. She handed him a glass of wine and then hooked her arm around his. He prayed he wouldn't spill all over her with the awkward position.

"To a lovely dinner," she said.

"Agreed," he returned.

They took a small sip with linked arms, and Flora broke into laughter.

"Yes?" Gregory asked.

"The arms linking always looked so fun in the movies, but really all the while I was worried I would either jostle your hand or you would make me spill wine down my dress."

He chuckled with her and forced himself to stop thinking about licking the trail of wine down her neck and into her cleavage. Instead he thought about whining kids. It helped to cool his ardor.

"I got a new client today," she said excitedly.

"Oh, yeah?" he asked.

He sat back as she launched into the details of her day. She was vibrant as she talked about her goals and the programming she would have to do. He watched her face light up as talked about being able to sustain her business and launched into talking about her other clients as well. Gregory nodded and smiled, not minding that he didn't understand half of the tech talk she was spouting. He enjoyed watching her talk about her passion.

"Oh, damn. The steak," she cried and leapt up.

Gregory stood and followed behind her. He feared he would have to choke down some hockey puck, but instead saw her standing with her hands fisted on her hips and staring at a plate.

"What can I carry to the table for you?" he asked.

"I actually planned to fix the plates here so we had enough table room," she said. "I'm sorry. These are going to be slightly unpalatable. I let them sit too long and now they are too cool."

"I don't mind, Flora," he said. "We can have slightly cool steak."

He thought he heard her mutter about her whole plan going askew but didn't ask her to clarify. He thought it cute the way she talked to herself.

"Want me to bring the wine glasses to the table?" he asked.

She nodded, and he went back to fetch the glasses. In the few seconds it took him to walk across the living room, she had set the plates and a decanter with the red wine on the table. She was finishing trip two with bowls of salad and a small round of bread. She leaned over to light candles and smiled at him.

Gregory walked over, held her chair, and then sat at the table. He bowed his head as she said grace and then looked into her warm, brown eyes.

"Thank you for dinner, Flora," he said.

"You are very welcome," she said.

He watched her take a small bite of beef and sigh in contentment. He took a quick drink of wine. The woman made the most erotic sounds when she really enjoyed something. Gregory wondered how she would sound beneath him. He took a bite of steak and moaned his own joy. Despite being a touch cool, it was cooked rare, and a light dusting of salt and pepper only served to enhance the satin beef taste.

"This is amazing," he said. "I love my steak rare."

"Me, too," she said. "I get crap all the time about it, but I don't care. And this is the good cut, from the farmer's market."

They made idle chat through dinner, and he found out that her favorite music changed by the day, her favorite season was summer, and her favorite color was blue. He smirked, but her sharply raised eyebrow stopped him before he made jokes about it. He told her about some of his tamer exploits with his friends through their high school years. To his surprise, he found himself talking about Marcus and explaining all his mentor had done to shape his life. Except the werewolf part. As a natural pause occurred, he thanked her for dinner again.

"I guess it's a good thing I changed my mind about serving turtle soup then," she teased.

"Well, darn, that is one of my favorites. Tastes like chicken," he said.

"Gregory! I thought…" she trailed off.

"I love turtles in all their forms, Flora Blu," he said, her name slipping over his lips like the fine wine he was drinking.

"What?"

Her eyes snapped to his, and he bit back a laugh. He watched Flora's eyes search his for a hint that he was teasing, but he gave her nothing.

"Let me help you clear the table?" he asked.

She nodded and then looked over her shoulder with a devious grin.

"Apparently, I called it right when I made devil's cake for you."

He watched her flounce back into the kitchen. He could imagine pressing against her and kissing over her silky shoulders. He wanted to press her against the counter and—Gregory's eyes snapped to his watch.

He had been there two hours, enjoying her company and food. His increasingly aggressive thoughts were a clear signal. The moon was rising higher in the sky, and it called to him. While he did not have to hunt, he did have to shift each night of the full moon. If he chose to wait too long, the choice would not be his. As much as he wanted to linger, he thought it might be safer to call it a night and get in his run.

She carried out a plate of dark, chocolate cake, and he decided he could stay a few minutes more. Gregory stared at the luscious piece of desert beckoning to him, but waited for his hostess. Flora bustled out to the kitchen and came in with another decanter of red wine. It was a deep maroon, purple color, and he could smell the blackberry notes.

"It's a Bandol from France," she explained.

Gregory smiled at her and decided to try it before deciding he would hate it. It went tremendously well with the cake, and he was satisfied as he finished his meal. Flora cooked simplistically, which he could appreciate. No sauces or fancy, toddler-sized portions. He had enjoyed the meal and even more so the company. He followed her back to the living room, and they sat listening to the music. From the huge windows of her loft, he could see the moon full and fat in the night sky. He turned to say something witty to her and instead fell into her warm eyes.

He leaned close to her and kissed her. He encountered no hesitation and slowly stroked her tongue with his. The soft feel and heat spiraled down and coiled tension in his stomach. Gregory put his hand on the small of her back, pressed Flora closer to him, and felt heat spike off of her as well. Her breasts pressed against his shirt, and he ran one hand down her side, over the ribs, and softly caressed the side of her breast. The beautiful, but damned, dress stopped him from touching smooth skin, and he cursed it.

"You melt my chocolate," she murmured against his lips.

He took that as the sign to kiss her harder and pressed against her as he lowered her back on the couch. She wrapped her hands around his neck and pulled him closer. The scent of her filled his nose, and he leaned down to nip a trail down her neck. She exhaled, and he captured her mouth again and kissed her until they both needed air. He ran his hand up her leg, and she dug fingernails into his arm. He leaned in to kiss her again, when the moonlight caught his eyes.

Gregory knew good and hell well that if he continued to romance Flora, things might take a lot longer than he had planned. Longer than he actually had. Still, he figured he could catch a run at three or four in the morning and still be okay. He was saved any other stupid, delay-tactic planning by the buzzing of his phone against his leg. He had forgotten that he had slipped it into his shorts pockets. He could bet that Travon was now blowing up his phone because Tess had told them about him skipping the run. And since he had not really filled in his brothers about Flora, there were questions to be answered. He mentally berated himself and slowly sat up. He hated the confusion in her eyes and tried to come up with something that would not sound…fantastical.

"Thank you so much for a lovely evening, Flora Blu," he said, pushing himself to his feet.

Gregory willed himself not to pull her up against him as she stood and smoothed her skirt.

"I'm sorry, I need to go. I just got an emergency text, and that means I need to leave."

"For-Mar needs you right now?"

"No," he said. "A friend needs me."

She tilted her head and pressed her lips together.

"Okay…well, if you have to," she said slowly.

"I promise to make it up to you soon. I just need to run," he said, feeling like an ass.

Gregory knew he should have postponed having dinner with her by at least a day, when it would have been safe. He also knew that any excuse had to be great or he would not have a chance with her again. He walked to the door and turned to press a light kiss against her lips.

"I had a great time. I am sorry I have to leave like this," he said. "I will call soon."

"Yeah, well, have a good night," she said. He didn't like the way she shut the door as soon as he passed the threshold. He scowled and jogged down the steps and out of the building. He would have to run hard to get over the frustration of his evening being interrupted. His phone buzzed again, and Gregory shut it off. It would be a long, lonely night.

Chapter 9

"Flora Blu Designs," she answered as she crawled under her desk to retrieve her mouse.

She smiled as the person on the other end was a new job offer. She carefully made it back to her seat, making sure she didn't smack her head as she exited. Flora grinned at the phone as details kept coming. She took quick notes, and her smile got wider. The caller, Deanna, had offered her a meeting that afternoon, because she wanted Flora to start as soon as possible. She managed not to squeal into the phone and was proud of how professional she sounded.

Flora hung up and then did squeal and dance around. She had until one that afternoon to get some basic notes mocked up, take a shower, and get ready to present her concepts for the project. Deanna owned a used book store in Holly. Her business had grown enough to need both a webstore, and an interactive inventory database for thousands of books. Flora took a quick look at the website and got a feel for the style and brand of her new client. The work would be pretty labor intensive as she collected the data and took inventory. At least with ISBN numbers, she wouldn't have to create a whole slew of product descriptions.

She went over all the different ideas that she could present. Overall, the job was pretty cut and dried; there was no sexy to sell for the webstore. There would be different styles of pages based on the genres of each book. Deanna also had a large, local author presence at her store and wanted nice pages for them as well. Flora wondered how hard it would be to rope the authors into posing for headshots, so they would be uniform.

A few hours later, Flora walked into Past Tense Books and smiled. It was the most comfortable and welcoming bookstore she had ever been in. The meeting with Deanna had been amazing and even fun. As they walked around the store, Flora took a few shots so she could incorporate the feel into the webstore. She paused by the local author display and smiled. It was nice when people got to pursue their passion. She picked up a book with a stunning cover in black matte.

"*Enter the Moon*," she murmured and then snorted. "Yeah, werewolves. I don't know how people can read this stuff."

Flora put it back down and after looking through, grabbed up a copy of *Sparrow* a contemporary romance and headed to the counter.

"Do the werewolf books really sell?" she asked, placing her purchase on the counter.

"They do really well. I can barely keep them stocked. You would love it. The author is amazing," Deanna said with a laugh. "Actually both authors are pretty cool. Hey, can I get a local author page that links to theirs as well? If you want, I'll ask the authors to give you their information."

Flora nodded and smiled.

"I can do contemporary romance, but paranormal? Not so much."

"Well, *Enter the Moon* is Urban Fantasy, so maybe that is more your style."

Flora snorted.

"It's about werewolves. No way."

She chatted with Deanna another twenty minutes, took notes, and promised to get a good start on the store and have a progress report in a week. She would need to look through her data and then start writing the code. As it was a Friday, she also reminded herself that she had promised to take the weekend off. Despite working for herself, Flora was determined to keep a sane work schedule and not burn herself out. She stepped out into the ninety-degree weather at eleven in the morning and sighed. Her phone buzzed, and she looked down and laughed at the eleven missed texts from Shonise.

She put on her headset and called her friend as she sat waiting for her car to cool down.

"Well?" Shonise demanded.

"I am fine, my new client is lovely, and despite living in an area that is as humid as a mouth, I am having a great day."

"Oh, girl. You are funny," Shonise drawled out. "You know darn well I just want to hear about the good parts. Get down to the details."

"We had dinner, and he brought me wine. Like four bottles of it, because he didn't know what I liked," Flora said.

"And?"

"The conversation was great, I messed up the steak and, yes, we kissed, and that is all," she said with a slight grimace. She had expected the evening to go much better and didn't understand just what had pulled him away.

"How was it?"

"It was good," she said.

"How good?"

"Well, if that little foot rub made me glow, I think I was positively luminous after his kisses this time," Flora said with a wide smile.

"Look at you, using a new word and all. One might think you have actually been paying attention when I talk," Shonise laughed.

"Look, Ms. English Teacher, my vocabulary is just fine. I mean, you might know a googolplex worth of words, but I'm the only one of us who is multi-lingual," she retorted.

"Really? You speak more than one language? And here I thought you only spoke English the same as me," her friend snorted. "I doubt either one of us has retained anything ninth grade French taught us."

"I speak SQL, Java, C++, PHP, and Python," Flora said proudly.

There was a deliberate pause.

"I'm sure you think what you just said made some sense, but I stopped listening as soon as you started talking geek."

"You are the worst friend ever," Flora grumbled.

"Nuh uh. I was smart enough to put condoms in your purse for you," Shonise said with a laugh. "Even though you didn't use them."

"You what? Why would you do something like that?"

"Because, unlike you, I can see where this is going with Gregory," Shonise said, very smugly. "And since I don't plan on being a god-mama just yet, I made sure you had something handy."

Flora tried not to take offense at her friend's tone of voice suggesting that her reasoning was the smartest conclusion to make about her relationship with Gregory.

"Well, I didn't anticipate it going that far," Flora said. "It was our first date. And then he up and left. No need for condoms.".''

"Girl, you are grown. If you like him, there is no reason not to enjoy him," Shonise scoffed. "Not to mention, this was at least date number four."

"I'm pretty sure I would remember having gone out another time with Gregory."

"The foot massage, the lunch date, and you walking through nature."

"I am very certain the disastrous run-in with nature does not count as a date," Flora knew her smile carried through her voice. "Well, this was the first real date. I don't count the one where Nature tried to kill me. We had a table and everything."

"Yeah, I will give you that. What do you mean he had to leave?"

Flora wrinkled her nose at the phone. She had hoped her friend would have missed that quick insertion.

"It was kind of weird, actually. We got into a great make-out session, all kissing and even some touching," Flora said. "But then, he got some text or something and said he needed to go."

"Maybe he was trying for the slow and sweet romance?" he friend asked.

"I don't think so. He just got up and left. He said he would call later this weekend."

"I wouldn't read anything into it," Shonise said. "If he doesn't call, then we go get him."

"There will be no hunting him down. I expect he will call tomorrow. Anyhow, I'm here at my office, and I have work to do."

"Later. Love you," Shonise said.

"Love you, too."

Seven days later, the heat had not abated and Flora steeled herself for the walk in the humidity from her car to her office. She managed not to melt into a puddle of sweat and got down to work. Despite her best plans, the Universe had decided that she and Gregory wouldn't see each other for another week. He had called like he promised, and they had made plans to have dinner at his house, which were canceled due to Flora's family throwing her great aunt a surprise, 95th birthday party. Their make-up lunch date was postponed due to his having an accident involving the mobile turtle van and a wild turkey. She had done her best not to laugh until she hung up.

To make it worse, their flirty texts had gotten more and more sexy. Flora really wanted to see him, but it just wasn't happening. Even her data collection trips had yielded no results of seeing him. The last time she texted that she would be at the center, he promised to be in touch soon. They had once again missed each other, so Flora dug into her projects.

Shaking her head, she pulled herself back to the work she needed to do. She kept busy until lunch, writing the program for the turtle database. She knew better than to jump into her new project. Her brain needed some days of planning space. It saved her time in the end because fewer revisions were needed. Flora was certain that once she got more shell samples, it would go smoothly, and barring any sort of craziness, she was done spending her fee. The thought made her just a bit giddy. She had been eyeing another suit from Gunnar's collection, not to mention the vacation to Louisville to go get it. She mentally roped Shonise in for the road trip and sat back with a smile. Her phone chimed, reminding her of her workout appointment, and she went to earn her glass of wine for the night.

After her dance class workout that tried but failed to kill her and a mostly satisfying lunch, Flora came back to her office. She closed the For-Mar project and opened up the program for Tri-Crescent Photography. She had been hired to create an e-newsletter for the ever growing client list. She smiled; she loved working with other small businesses in the area. They all went through the same struggle, and it was nice to see when others started doing well. It didn't hurt that they also did her biography photo for her own website. She opened up the code and began to update the program to include the new opt-in or opt-out strings. Most people hated giving out email addresses because of spam mails, and the owner decided he would rather have the clients willingly receiving messages about his latest deals and specials.

Ninety minutes later, Flora mopped sweat from her brow with her handkerchief and then stopped and looked at it. She finally realized that she was dripping sweat down her back, and when she stood, the leather on her chair was shiny.

"Crap, the air must be out," she moaned.

She walked over to the thermostat; her office was a toasty eighty-seven degrees. As she reached over her desk for her cell phone, the lights went out. Flora sighed and blew out a frustrated stream of air. She knew it was a brownout from the heat levels, and as she got ready to call and add her name to the complaint list for Consumer's Energy, she heard a pop and a click. Her eyes rounded, and she looked at the bright blue screen of death facing her. Despite having a backup system to ensure her computer would run for a full thirty minutes after a power shut-off, she knew the motherboard just went sideways on her.

"Calm down, Flora. We routinely back things up," she reminded herself. "We can just pop the hard drive and plug it in at home. It will be fine."

Her phone rang on top of the desk, and the vibrations patted her head in a condescending manner.

"Hi, Momma. Yes, the power is out at my office. No, I have no idea if I have power at home. Yes, I will come stay with you and Daddy if it's out. Love you, too."

She grinned at her mother's keeping tabs on her. She crawled further under her desk, using her phone as a light source, and grumbled at herself as she pulled the tower out. She opened it, and dust bunnies flew at her face.

"Well, Flora, apparently dusting needs to be on the weekly schedule," she snarked at herself. "But then again, it doesn't matter when things decide they are going to die. And eat up hours of work."

She climbed out from under her desk, mad. She understood most people wouldn't think about computer maintenance or even know how to do it, but it was her livelihood and she knew better. She stood, hard drive in hand, ready to leave, and looked around the dark office. Flora sighed in loud disgust about her plans being derailed. The one good thing about cloud service was that most of her work should be backed up. She grabbed her keys and headed out the door.

She walked back into her nicely cooled apartment ten minutes later. She went into the spare room/office and turned on her laptop. She plugged in the hard drive as an external slave drive and walked out to get a drink. She wished she could have an adult beverage but knew it might just put her to sleep.

"The whole point of paying for office space is to have that whole separation of home and work spaces," she grumped as she headed for the fridge.

Walking back into the office, Flora sipped her lemonade. She sat at her desk, ready to work on her file, and wanted to cry as she opened the Tri-Crescent folder. None of her hard work could be found. She supposed she could be happy that only the updates were missing and that the whole file wasn't corrupted, but with the heat and the brownout, she didn't feel like the glass-half-full type of girl in that moment. Still, she settled down and cranked out work for a full four hours before her neck and back screamed at her. She squinted at the clock and nodded to herself. It was six o'clock so she could be done, but she was determined to finish the file before allowing herself to find an old television show to marathon.

Her laptop blinked a lazy red light at her, and she sighed.

"Of course you need to be plugged in, because why would I actually take care of my tech today?" she asked the Universe.

She grabbed the plug and carefully placed it into the wall. The last thing she needed was for a fit to cause a power surge or something stupid. Flora walked back to her kitchen for another glass of lemonade. Of all the many things she loved about her mother; she was particularly happy that she had been forced to learn how to make real lemonade. It beat the pants off the powdered mix any day. She walked back to her office, planning to put in her last twenty minutes of work.

The lights went out, and Flora cursed a streak that would shock the dear pastor who had been so happy to see her praying a few days before. She really had not planned on having a sleepover at her parents. She scowled at the darkness.

"I just want to finish my work and then relax!" she shouted into the air.

She sat down at her desk just in time to see her computer blink off. Flora refused to cry.

"Right, because my battery has been dying for almost two whole weeks, and I haven't managed to order a new one, yet," she said. "Because why order a battery when you can just plug the damn thing in? I swear, technological procrastination will be the death of me."

Her phone rang and stopped the spiral of self-recrimination before it got too bad.

"You dark?"

"Yes, and both computers died," she whined at her friend.

"Great."

"It is not great, Shonise. This is my livelihood."

"You promised you would start taking weekends off. Apparently, someone up there was listening and is forcing you to do what you said. So, get your mopey self ready. There is a jazz band playing at Kearsley and I want to go have fun."

"Not like I can do anything else today," Flora conceded. "Let me get changed."

She smiled as her best friend again promised a fun time dancing. Each season, "Music in the Parks" hosted some amazing musical talent, for free, at various parks around the Genesee County area. Flora had learned about the program in college, where her friends insisted that she join them. Aside from Shonise, Flora didn't really have a lot of close friends, so when she found a few more women to hang out with in college, she tried to be adventurous. To her surprise, she really enjoyed the free concerts and tried to get to some of the concerts each year. Even more, she always tried to reconnect with her friends if she could.

Flora looked through her closet out of habit and chose the lightest outfit she could think of because it would be damn hot despite the concert starting at seven in the evening. She pulled out her white sundress with flowers and dug out her tan wedges—clean from their excursion at For-Mar—and nodded.

She looked in the mirror and forced a smile onto her lips. She might not dance a lot, because of the warm evening, but she would go, forget about the rotten past few hours, and have a good time. Or she would die trying.

Chapter 10

Gregory wiped the sweat off his face and waved as Travon took the last group back to the bus. He loved watching city kids get immersed in nature for the first time. He also got distinct joy from working with Travon and his group from Big Brothers and Big Sisters of Flint. The kids were well behaved but curious about everything. He enjoyed showing them the wild raspberry and blackberry bushes along the hiking trails. They had a long conversation about how food was grown and how it eventually made it to the store. He knew that the community garden program was still in place, but it was different when it came to sweet, ripe fruit. Nothing beat the juicy taste of fresh off the bushes. Even better, the kids' leaving meant he could start his weekend. His last run solo during the full moon cycle had been very fulfilling, as it was already good to reconnect with his natural self. However, Gregory was ready to relax, work on the addition to his cabin, and have peace and quiet.

He walked into the small office of the visitor's center and filled out his paperwork as quickly as possible. It was still hot outside, and he wanted to be out of the stuffy building as soon as he could. He grabbed his bike and made his way home in a mere fifteen minutes. Gregory leaned the bike against his house and shed clothes as he walked to the lake. It was the kind of hot and humid day that made him appreciate his home. He walked into the lake without hesitation and sighed in contentment as he finally made it up to his neck in the cool liquid.

Treading water in a lazy pattern, he let his mind wander around his day and into a quiet meditation, allowing him to come down from his week. It was Friday, and he had no pressing plans for the next two days. He planned a leisurely night of grabbing dinner and a cold beer or two and then a weekend spent either reading or perhaps getting around to his carpentry project. Marcus had introduced him to basic construction when he brought him into the pack. It had been the perfect way to reign in a group of teenagers who had just learned about their heritage. It was also a really great skill to have when you needed extra money. Gregory swam twenty laps from where he could stand, around the floating raft, and back. He pushed himself harder, and when his labored breathing made him choke on yet another mouthful of water, he called it quits.

He strode out of the water, crouched down by his trap, and grabbed out two fish for his dinner.

"Dude, you have got to start wearing shorts."

"Hey, Tray. What are you doing here?"

"Asking you about missing the hunt last week," his friend said. "Other than running into you at work, I haven't seen or heard from you. What's up?"

"I had other plans that night. Which Tess knew, and it was why she dropped I wasn't running the hunt. I'm pissed she involved you guys," he said with a scowl. "As for the last week, I've just been busy."

"She knew? She asked around for you like you were supposed to be there or something. It's why I texted you," Travon said. "She's being petty and jealous. I thought she broke up with you."

"Yes, she did. Apparently, it was fine with her to be broken up, until I got a date," Gregory said. "Anyhow, now that you have your answer, do you want some dinner?"

"No way, son. I am taking your boring, soon-to-be-dressed ass out for some fun," Travon said.

"I am having fun. I had a nice dip in the lake and am about to grill this fish and drink a beer. What more do I need?" asked Gregory.

"A night out with your friends," Tray said. "You owe us some details about this chick you are seeing. What kind of shit is it that we had to hear from Tess?"

Gregory wanted to laugh as his friend walked ahead of him back to the house. Considering how many times they had seen each other shift back and forth, it made no sense that his friend would have any reaction to seeing him naked.

"So, this urge to make sure I hang out with you all is the reason you are dragging me out?"

"Yes."

"What is the reason you rushed ahead of me? Are you carefully not looking at my well-toned ass?" Gregory said, poking at his friend.

"I have seen your ass more than I will ever admit, and it does nothing for me. Now, if you will kindly get it into some shorts, we can go meet the others. We are going to hear some jazz and then catch some eats and drinks."

"You know, we could do that here," Gregory started.

"No deal. This is live jazz," Travon said. "We hang out a lot here, and it's great. But, G, we all need a change of scenery. Not to mention, it's hard for me to pick up the ladies here when there are none.

I mean, you got your mystery outing that you just refuse to talk about and all."

Gregory ignored him and headed in to take a shower. Fifteen minutes later, with lawn chairs in hand, they met up with Matthias and Nathaniel. Despite Tray's offer, Gregory drove on his own. He loved his friend, but he knew better than to strand himself to the whims to said friend who was determined to get himself a hook-up for the night. He knew all the guys still wanted some details about his date, but after learning that Tess had set him up, he wasn't in the mood to share. Gregory had been telling Tess the truth when he said he was okay with it being over. He certainly hoped she had moved on. It was a nice, winter diversion, but there was no future with her. He was slated to be the next pack Alpha, and despite her holding the Beta position, he had no intention of spending forever with her.

He set up his chair and then went to greet his boys. He walked up, man-hugged Mathias, and caught money passing hands between Travon and Nathaniel. He turned his head and cast a questioning glance at Tray, who shrugged and smiled.

"Really?"

"Sure. I needed the twenty, and rich boy here fell for it."

"Because I never come out with you all?"

Gregory shook his head, but before he could retort, the announcer came on and introduced the group. The crowd, already rowdy and restless from the heat, cheered loudly, and the music began. The enthusiasm was infectious, and after a few songs, Gregory danced along in its thrall. He was moving with the beat and scanning the crowd. A wide smile covered her face when he saw Flora dancing across the lawn with another lady. His eyes trailed over her white sundress with bright pink and yellow flowers on the skirt. He grinned to himself as he noted that she wore the same shoes as she had on the first day he had met her. He raised his arm to wave at her. She didn't return it, so he hoped that she just hadn't seen him, instead of the possibility that she was ignoring him.

"Who is she?" Nathaniel asked loudly in his ear.

"My date from last Thursday night. The database programmer that For-Mar just hired to catalogue my turtles," Gregory said. Then catching the look from his friend, he laughed. "Really, 'Thaniel, we do not live in the Dark Ages. Women are computer programmers, too."

"Not ones who look like that," his friend insisted.

"This one does, and if you will excuse me, I am going to say hello."

Gregory pushed by his friend, shaking his head. He had walked about ten paces away when his friend called out.

"Introduce me to her friend."

"No way," he said, without looking back. "You know the rule."

When the foursome had been teenagers, they had made a pact that they would not hook each other up with friends of their dates. Arrangements like that could get messy, and when a couple broke up, it would put other friends of friends in weird places. A few times that rule had been broken, and it had gotten ugly. Then again, Gregory reflected, the problem usually started and stopped with Nathaniel. He had a way with words that made women want to kill him in the slowest and most painful way possible. There was no way he would set up Flora's friend and then have to hear about it.

He wove his way through the pulsing and dancing crowd in time to the music. It was still warm out, but people still swayed and moved as they appreciated the music. He made it to Flora and decided he would dance with her and not interrupt the rhythm she had going. He slid behind her and smiled when her friend gave him a pointed stare and raised an eyebrow at him. Gregory leaned in close to Flora's ear.

"I love this song," he said.

He would have preferred it to be a sexy whisper; however, at an outside concert, there was no other way to be heard. He grinned at her as her head whipped around in surprise. He wanted to kiss her after she gave him a saucy wink. Instead, he contented himself with placing his hands on her hips as she swayed.

"I thought you said you were going to call," Flora said.

"No, I said I would be in touch," he said with a smile. "And I do believe this is touching."

Slowly, he rotated her to face him and felt the heat of a wicked and crooked grin accompany the once-over she gave him all the way in his groin. Gregory wanted to lean in and kiss her, but the band decided to move into a faster paced song, and the crowd danced along with it. As he moved against, with, and around Flora, he was very aware of her body. With each step she took, he countered it and blocked her from moving too far away from him. As the last song was announced, he stepped the game up. He made it a clear seduction through movements, and she responded. The crowd fell away from his vision as he moved with her.

As they swayed in time with the music and each other, he gave in and kissed her. It was heated and sexy as his mouth slanted against hers. The loud cheering of the crowd startled him slightly as he had almost forgotten they existed. The band said their good-nights, and people started to leave the park.

"I'm not ready for the night to end," Flora said, looking at him. "It was a long week without seeing you."

"How about a moonlight swim?" he asked. "It will help to break this heat."

The moon was waning but was still full enough that it would give off enough light for them to swim by. Flora nodded her head, and he was very happy that he had driven himself. He clasped her hand in his and gave her enough time to prattle off an excuse to her friend before giving it a gentle tug. He walked by his group of friends to grab his chair and waved. He grinned and promptly ignored all raised eyebrows and shade thrown his way. No words were spoken as he opened the car door for her and tossed his chair in the back. It took ten minutes of being on the road before anything was said.

"I really didn't expect to see you there," Flora said.

"Yeah, periodically I leave For-Mar," he grinned. "My friends were pretty determined to drag me out for fun tonight. I suppose I should probably thank them."

Her giggle made him smile in response.

"Yes, Shonise insisted I come out tonight, but she only got her way because both my computers were down and the lights cut off."

"So even your technology wanted you to take a night off?" he questioned. "I'm surprised you would be working on a Friday night."

"I work when I have programs to complete," she said with a shrug. "My business is still new to the area, which means I work all sorts of hours. Someday, when I am big enough to have minions, I will let them take the weekend hours, but for now it's just me."

"I am glad," he said.

"You are?" Flora asked, turning to face him.

Her profile against the dark sky just begged him to kiss her.

"Yes. If you had minions, I would have never met you."

He turned down the dirt road leading to his home and, in a few moments, parked and jumped out to open her door. Gregory led her into his house.

"Oh, I think your electricity went out, too," she said.

"No, I see my kitchen light on," he said.

"But it's warm in here. Is your air out?" she asked.

He wanted to laugh, but her voice held dismay. To buy himself time, Gregory walked around and opened the window. The cross-breeze helped the small, wood cabin cool quickly.

"I don't have air conditioning here," he explained. "The cross-breeze usually does a good job of keeping the house at a nice temperature."

He grabbed her hand again and led her to the back deck. As she looked up into the dark sky dotted with stars, he watched and marveled at her soft profile.

"Beautiful," she murmured.

"I agree," he said, knowing his compliment wasn't lost on her when she turned and met his eyes. "Can I get you a drink?"

"Do you have wine?" she asked.

"Sure. Red or a nice, chilled rose," he offered.

She asked for rose, and he walked to the corner of the deck where his outdoor fridge sat and poured her a glass. He grabbed himself a beer and made his way back to her side. He took a couple of sips and watched her survey the surroundings.

"You live out in the middle of the woods?" she asked. "Can I be sure you aren't an axe murderer?"

"Well, it would be a bit late to ask now," he chuckled. "And I live about fifteen minutes from Courtland. So, not out in the sticks but back off the road far enough to enjoy the quiet. It's a private lake, and there are only ten homes surrounding it."

They sat in comfortable quiet for a few moments, and then he heard a muffled curse and a sharp slap of her hand against skin. He shook his head; the heat drove mosquitos out in ravaging, blood-sucking squadrons. He held his hand out to her in silence, and they walked into his place. The living room boasted a nice, large fireplace that was shared with the kitchen and some comfortably broken-in sofas. There were three bookshelves and a couple of lamps.

"Raincheck on the swim?"

"Maybe. Do you have a pool?"

He laughed and shook his head.

"Just the lake."

"No thanks, then."

"Would you like another drink?" he asked as he led her to the couch.

"Not really," she said.

She looked up at him from hooded eyes. Gregory leaned his head in close and slowly kissed her. He had read the signs correctly as she returned the kiss and snuggled into him. He sat next to her and pulled her in closer. To his surprise, Flora pressed into him and took the kiss from a gentle press to exploring and hot. Her tongue slicked against his, making his heart race. Her fingers alternately splayed across his chest and curled into his shirt as she kissed him.

"Off," she murmured against his lips.

It took him a moment to realize she was tugging at his shirt. He broke the kiss and began to nuzzle down the side of her neck as he unbuttoned his shirt. Her hands pressed against his flesh with a scorching touch. The pads of her fingers ran over his chest, and his nipples hardened in response. Her tiny touches aroused him, and he grabbed her wrists to still them.

"Flora?" he questioned.

"Gregory?" she rasped back.

"If you keep touching me like that…" he started.

"We will end up in your bed?" she asked. "Because that is where I hoped it would lead."

He blinked at her very clear answer and then smiled at her. He had begun to lead her to the bedroom, when she grabbed her purse. She pulled out a foil packet and smiled at him triumphantly. Gregory blinked in slight surprise. He hadn't really thought about protection in that moment and was glad that she had. As timid as Flora was about her work at For-Mar, she certainly seemed to have no problem about being an equal in the bedroom.

In his room, he kissed her again slowly, moving from her lips down the side of her neck and to her shoulder. As his lips made a trail around her shoulder, he slowly slid the strap of her dress down. His hands worked at the zipper on the back and then on her bra strap. He slid his palms down her rib cage, cupped her nicely rounded bottom, and pulled her against him. To his surprise, she nipped at his collarbone before pushing him away enough to work at the zipper of his shorts.

"I think this is the best possible outcome of the evening," she said with a wink at him. "I was pretty certain I would be going home and eating up the ice cream before it melted in my not-running freezer."

He started to laugh and offer her the ice cream from his freezer, but she grabbed his shaft in one warm hand and he stopped thinking about anything more than sinking into her. Gregory made short work of the rest of their clothes, though he couldn't stop himself from lavishing some attention to her tightly budded, chocolate nipples with his tongue. He lowered her to the bed and continued to kiss her body. She exhaled in a lusty sigh, but he continued the slow exploration up and down her.

Gregory all but jumped when she ran her fingernails over his flat nipples as he touched her and scored them just enough to make them stand to attention. She pulled his head down for a kiss. He heard a slight ripping noise and felt the smooth latex sheath him. He grinned down at her and held her eyes as he entered her. Her legs clamped around his waist, and Gregory realized that she wanted to lead the pace, which was fine with him. He rolled them over so that she sat on top and met each thrust and drive with equal passion. He grabbed onto her hips and drove upward as his orgasm thundered through him. He heard her cry out before she fell against his chest.

They lay kissing in each other's embrace, and eventually he got up. He pulled on a pair of shorts and brought her a t-shirt.

"That was an amazing warm-up," Flora said, pulling the shirt over her head.

He turned with a smile, drinking in the sight of her. His t-shirt reached mid-thigh on her, and she stood with her head tilted, looking at him. He laughed at her saucy attitude.

"Indeed, it was a great warm-up. How about a nice, cold glass of tea before we retire for the night?" he asked.

She nodded and sat back on the bed. Gregory walked out and grabbed the pitcher of tea from his fridge, shaking his head. Delicate, sexy, and feisty all rolled into one sweet package that made up Flora Blu. A night breeze passed through the house, cooling it, but Gregory knew there would be more heat that night and planned to enjoy every moment of being with her.

Chapter 11

Flora slowly became aware of someone kissing her neck. It sent shivers through her body. She peeked her eyes open and slowly rolled over. Gregory didn't lose a beat and started kissing down her shoulders, making his way towards her sheet-covered breasts. She grinned and pulled his lips up to meet hers in a heated kiss. His tongue stroked against hers as his hand began stroking her thigh. She moaned into his mouth, but before she could let anything else happen, her bladder reminded her that it was morning.

"Where are you facilities?" she asked.

She blushed as he chuckled.

"Facilities? Really, Flora Blu, you just spent all night with me in a variety of positions of pleasure and you can't ask for the bathroom?"

Flora rolled her eyes at him and walked in the direction he pointed, but stopped and looked over her shoulder at him.

"Positions of pleasure? Seriously, Gregory? And you had the nerve to laugh at my word choices? My best friend teaches English, she's all Ms. Formal all the time. I guess it is brushing off one me."

Flora sauntered into the bathroom and, after reliving herself, smiled at her reflection as she washed her hands. There certainly had been many positions, and no matter what word she might choose, she glowed. She walked back and sat on the corner of the bed. She said nothing as she looked at Gregory, almost as if trying to memorize each line of physique. His body was nice and toned, evident that he spent a lot of time moving. He had clearly defined muscles, but what captured her attention the most were his deep, soulful eyes. The rich caramel color drew her in each time she met them. They mesmerized her. Flora wanted to snort for even thinking the word, but he had a definite effect on her.

"What are your plans for the day?" she asked.

His response was to move closer and the bedsheet so carefully draped around his hips slid lower. Flora took in the sleekly muscled line of his hip and his taut stomach. She figured he must do more crunches than she ever planned to for those lines, but she appreciated his dedication. He crooked a finger at her. She scooted further onto the bed, sat near the headboard, and looked at him.

"Were you thinking of showing me another position of pleasure?" she said and then started to laugh.

The laugh tapered off as she watched him roll over and reach toward his night table. Not that she minded the view of his very well-toned buttocks. She noted that they were as nicely tanned as the rest of his body and made note to inquire about it. He held up a small bottle of oil and nodded that she should lay back. She could smell lavender as his strong fingers found the arch of her foot and began to massage it. She relaxed further into the bed to enjoy the sensation of his touch. She sighed as the massage managed to both ease and create pressure in her.

"I think you should perhaps rethink your footwear, Flora Blu," he said. "You carry a lot of tension in your feet."

Flora meant to make a snarky reply but instead exhaled softly as his lips found her ankle and kissed a trail upward until they reached her mid-thigh. He looked directly at her, meeting and holding her gaze as he continued to touch her. He winked and began on the other leg, massaging her foot and trailing kisses up her thigh. He gentle indicated for her to roll over.

A soft dripping of oil on her back made her realize how sensitive her entire body had become from his touches. He started from the base of her neck and worked his way down her lower back, alternating touches from his fingers and the palm of his hand, repeating the motions several times over and changing his stroke with each cycle up and down her body.

Before she could get used to one particular sensation, he alternated between using wide, circular movements with his palm to using firm pressure with his fingertips just under her shoulder blades. She felt a rush of heat when he raked his fingernails down the insides of her thighs and could not believe just how erotic tickling could feel when he moved up and down her spine. The nerves in her entire body were saturated with pleasurable stimulation. A deep, earthy moan escaped her body unbidden when he began to stroke the length of her body. He started in the middle of her back and worked one hand up towards her neck, the other hand moving down towards her ankle.

Just when Flora thought she had gone through all the sensations, Gregory used light, teasing movements with his fingertips along her rib cage. She couldn't even muster a giggle, because the riot of sensations was moving her towards a much more satisfying conclusion. She was only slightly surprised when he began touching her buttocks. He squeezed the cheeks together, moving them in a circular motion, and then spread them slightly apart. Lavender filled her nose, and the hairs on her arms rose.

As he touched and stimulated her with his hands, Flora shivered under each kiss he placed up and down her entire spine. A gentle bite on her back made her arch off the bed. She gripped the sheets as a teasing lick here and there made her shudder. He ran his lips softly against the skin she swore was on fire. The moan that slipped from her lips was deep. The gentle pressure was enhanced by the long, languid strokes he used up and down her legs.

"Gregory," she sighed.

He gently rolled her over and met her eyes.

"Flora?" he questioned.

"Now," she demanded.

Gregory complied by dipping his head between her thighs and brought her to a screaming orgasm with firm strokes of his fingers and tongue in a rapid, staccato beat. She pushed against his shoulders as the sensation threatened to overwhelm her. She felt warmth envelop her as he crawled up behind her and cuddled her close. He continued to touch and stroke her, keeping her aroused. He nudged her thighs apart, resting one on top of his as he entered her in a gentle slide.

Flora gripped his arms encircling her, and he moved with her into a frenetic haze of passion. The sensations rode through her as she gasped from the force of him. She lost her conscious self to the waves of the pleasure, not caring one second if she drowned in them. To her great delight, she heard his shout of release seconds after hers and wilted back against him. She felt him brush a gentle kiss just under her ear. Exhaustion beckoned, and she followed it, sated.

Flora again woke to Gregory kissing her shoulder.

"Would you like some brunch?" he asked softly.

"What happened to breakfast?" she asked with a giggle.

"Well, I had my breakfast," he chided.

Flora felt a blush cover her face and ground her backside against him. She smiled as he groaned.

"And here I was hoping to return the lovely massage you gave me," she said. "Those definitely are your strong point."

"Woman, I need some sustenance before we do anything else," he muttered.

She laughed then, and he kissed between her shoulder blades. She rolled over and kissed him properly. It started gentle and satisfying, but she inched in closer as his tongue stroked hers and her stomach coiled in anticipation. She pushed against his shoulder as her stomach grumbled at being empty.

"Okay, our human frailty conspires against us," she said against his warm lips. "Let's go find some brunch. Can I have one of your t-shirts? I didn't pack an overnight bag."

She rolled over onto her side and propped herself up, resting her head on her hand and blatantly staring at him as he strode over to a beautifully carved, wood dresser. He held up a plain, white t-shirt and a faded, red and black, football jersey.

"Yours?" she asked.

"Yeah, from when I played at Central," he said.

Gregory turned it around where she saw *Bell* across the top and the number 11. She walked over and took it from him. He pulled her in for another kiss, and they both laughed as his stomach did the rumbling.

"I suppose I can wear it, no matter what it looks like," she said. "I will need some boxers, too."

"What are your colors?" he asked.

"Blue and grey," she said proudly.

"Carmen-Ainsworth?" he snorted.

Flora squared her shoulders. "What of it?"

She stared at Gregory as he walked over to her and kissed her forehead, nose, and then lips.

"I heard you all were snooty, but I see I heard wrong," he said.

"Good answer," she laughed.

She dressed quickly and followed him out to the kitchen. She watched as he pulled out bread, bacon, and even a bowl full of blueberries. She admired his backside as he leaned over further and rummaged around.

"Damn, I need to go grab some eggs," he said.

"Well, if you have to run to the store, why don't we just go out for brunch?" she asked.

"No need. The henhouse isn't too far," he said.

"Henhouse?" she asked, certain she had not heard him correctly.

"Yes," he laughed gently. "A few of us that live around the lake decided that raising chickens couldn't be that hard. We built a henhouse and currently have about thirty chickens. It's close by. It won't take me long."

"Okay, henhouse…" she said, not sure what to make of it.

"You do know eggs come from chickens?" he teased.

"Of course I do. I just have never met anyone who raised chickens," she said.

"Well, now you have," he said.

Flora shook her head and ran a finger over his arm. She stood on tiptoe and kissed him.

"Let me get those eggs so we can go back to more interesting things," he said.

"Right," Flora said, patting him on the butt when he walked by.

She giggled and he raised an eyebrow at her. The giggles turned into full-blown laughter as he shook his head and, not quite under his breath, promised her a spanking but still left the house. She peeked out the door and watched as he walked around the lake. She couldn't even see the henhouse and wondered what he considered 'not long' in terms of her having to wait. All kidding and kissing aside, she was very hungry. She looked around a few times and then decided that the least she could do was get some coffee started.

Flora easily found the coffee maker on the counter but didn't see any coffee. She started looking through his cupboards, not at all feeling bad about being nosy, since it was the only way she was going to get her caffeine fix. So far, she had found dishes, more gallons of vinegar than she could make sense of, and a crockpot, but no coffee.

"Excuse me."

Flora prided herself for not shrieking and messing herself when she heard the strange voice. She turned to find a tall woman standing behind her in the kitchen like she owned it. They gave each other a pointed look-over. Flora admired the dark auburn locs the woman wore but didn't care for the skimpy, spaghetti strap tank top and barely-there shorts. After the woman gave her a once-over, their eyes met. The woman turned her back, reached into a cupboard, and produced a jar of coffee beans.

"I'm Tess," she said. "Sorry to scare you. Gregory and I often share coffee in the morning. Do you mind if I make a pot?"

"No. Go ahead," Flora said.

She watched Tess strut around the kitchen and wanted to slap her. It was evident that she was very familiar with the room and was comfortable being there as she easily pulled out a coffee grinder. Once the noise subsided, she bristled as Tess gave her a quick glance over her shoulder, again taking in the jersey and boxers she wore. She straightened her spine. If the woman wanted some confrontation, she would be happy to provide some. She went to the fridge, crowding the woman's space in the kitchen.

"Do you take milk?" she asked sweetly.

"Nope. I like it strong and black," Tess countered.

Flora bit back some curse words that formed in her mind. The double entendre wasn't lost on her. Nothing else was said until the coffee stopped dripping into the pot. Despite all the names Flora had been calling Tess in her mind, the brew smelled delicious. She reached up to grab a mug.

"That one is mine," Tess said.

Flora handed the mug to Tess and reached for another. She took a quiet deep breath and moved over to the counter to add a healthy dose of milk. Sadly, she didn't see any sugar and braced herself to deal with the Amazon dominating the kitchen.

"Where is the sugar?" she asked, keeping her voice pitched to be kind.

"For what?" Tess asked.

Flora interpreted the look that she was given as "you poor, stupid thing" and tried not to look shocked as a glass jar with some amber liquid was shoved toward her.

"Try the maple syrup. It's what we use," Tess said. "It goes much better with the home-roasted beans."

"Thanks, but I really like sugar."

"It's in the left-hand cupboard next to the stove," Tess said with a shrug of her shoulders.

Flora took the sugar bowl, added a big spoonful, and stirred it slowly. Despite being a bitch, Tess did know how to make a great cup of coffee. Obviously, there had been something between Gregory and the woman, but she gave Gregory credit for not being a cheater. Flora walked back over to the couch and sat. She tucked her feet under her and sipped from her mug. And made the huge mistake of thinking that Tess would leave.

Instead, the woman stood across from her and sipped her coffee, as well. Flora knew something stupid was about to be said.

 "So, where did you and Gregory meet?"

"At For-Mar," Flora said.

"Oh, of course you did," Tess nodded. "Women do love a man in uniform."

Flora said nothing and sat there. She had hoped the woman would just leave, but apparently there was no intention of going. She didn't quite understand why Tess would just hang around.

"When will Gregory return?" Tess asked her.

"I'm not sure. He went to the henhouse," Flora said.

To her surprise, Tess laughed and shook her head.

"Wow. He is pulling out all the stops for you. Funny, he didn't even tell me he had started dating someone else," she said and then shrugged her shoulders. "Then again, it's more of a courtesy than a rule."

Flora didn't like the implications of what she was hearing. She tried to stay calm and just drink the coffee. It lasted about two seconds.

"What you are not so subtly hinting at is that you and Gregory are seeing each other?" she asked.

"It's a casual thing," Tess said. "Not like I have any claims or anything. I was just surprised to see you here. Usually, he says something when he is dating, but he said nothing when we hung out last Thursday. Anyhow, this is getting awkward, so I'm going to head home. Thanks for the coffee."

Tess gave her a pithy smile as she placed her mug in the sink and then walked out of the house. Flora stood and walked to the door. She watched the woman stroll across the lawn at a leisurely pace. She tried her best not to be pissed off, but she couldn't help it. She took off his clothes, and as she zipped up her sundress, doubt flooded her mind. Gregory had left suddenly Thursday night and then hadn't said anything about it. Granted, they had texted through the week; however, Flora had never once thought to ask about what had happened.

Her mind climbed through a myriad of what might have happened. She wanted to give Gregory the benefit of the doubt, but Tess's comfort in his home put big doubt in her mind. She didn't want to believe that he could possibly be a liar and cheat. But she didn't know, because their conversations had never gone into talking about their ex's. She desperately hoped she was wrong about him. As if summoned by thought, he came back into her view. He smiled at her as he got closer, and she returned the smile as best she could.

"Eggs," he said with a flourish and showed her six brown eggs as he walked in the house.

She watched him walk into the kitchen.

"Glad you found the coffee," he said.

"Yeah," she said, and despite knowing that Tess was a bitch and meant to cause trouble, Flora needed to know why he had left.

She stood behind him as he opened the cupboard. It was a chicken move, but she doubted she could ask him if they had eye contact.

"Gregory, I have a question about Thursday night."

Chapter 12

Gregory felt a cold ball knot in his stomach with her question. He stared straight ahead and took a deep breath. With the nice pace the morning had set, the question came from nowhere. As he grabbed a mug for coffee, the answer made itself clear. The brown and yellow mug with the owls was missing, meaning that Flora hadn't made the coffee; Tess had. His brain spun as he tried to figure out what to say, because he couldn't see any way that this conversation would end well.

"What's your question?" he said as he poured the coffee.

Gregory wanted to pour a healthy shot of whiskey into his coffee. Their talk could only go from tense to terrifying. He turned to face her and noticed she didn't return the smile he gave her. He nodded toward Flora's mug, and she held it out for a warm-up. Gregory tried to make eye contact again, but she seemed busy avoiding him. Looking at her again, he noticed that she was fully dressed. In her own clothes. Finally, she met his eyes.

"Why did you leave Thursday night? It seemed like everything was going really well. And then all of a sudden, you left."

"I had business to attend to," he said. "I didn't plan for it, but I got those texts and it was something I had to take care of."

"Well, what business?" she pressed.

Gregory bought himself a few seconds by taking a good, long drink of coffee. He tried to figure out how to make it not sound like a lame-ass excuse. He put the mug down and turned to face Flora. He could see the tension in her face and wanted to hug her close.

"It's not something I can talk about, Flora. There are privacy concerns," he said simply.

"Were you with Tess?"

The question hung in the air between them. Gregory paused a few seconds too long and could see the damage those precious ticks of time had cost him. His mind raced to find an answer that might work. Her wide, brown eyes bored into him, and he felt a sinking sensation.

Yes, he had seen Tess that night. After having his phone blown up with concerned texts from his friends, Gregory had left Flora's apartment and gone to the meeting site. He had found Travon, Nathaniel, and Mathias anxious to see him. They had rushed over to him, concern evident on their faces. He hugged each one in turn and then faced them as a group.

"Man, I thought you had gotten trapped or something," Travon had said in greeting.

His friends were agitated. The full moon was calling them, and the need to change was getting stronger. For a moment, Gregory had been relieved that he had had to leave. It would be great to run with his friends.

"Why?" Gregory had asked. "I just didn't plan to hunt tonight. But I know better than not to shift. I definitely planned to go on a run later."

An odd look passed between his friends, and Gregory stared at them until they began to fidget. He waited, and eventually the others stared at Travon, making him the default fall guy.

"We just started to get worried," Travon said, clearly confused. "Not for nothing, but you haven't missed a hunt in years. You didn't answer our texts, either. So, where were you?"

"I was busy," Gregory had said. "There is no rule about having to hunt each month."

"You don't need to be a jerk. We were worried something had happened to you," Mathias said. "We care about you."

There were looks thrown and general grumbling about his sour mood, but he said nothing as he shrugged his shoulders and stripped to get ready for the run. The hunt that night had been a great stress release, lots of running and chasing. No one had actually caught a deer. The kill from the night before had made them rather *laissez-faire* about it. Once the hunt was over, the rest of them had gone back to Nathaniel's for an impromptu party.

"You're not coming?" Nathaniel had scowled.

"Not in the mood," he said, already walking away from them.

He remembered being highly irritated that his friends had ruined his date and wanted to go home to sulk. The words his friends had for him weren't even grumbled under their breath. They were said loud and clear at his back, moving him along even faster. Gregory hadn't thought much past that night, but he had not imagined a week later it could come back to bite him in the ass. Standing in his kitchen, irritation gave way to anger as he realized just what trouble Tess had caused. He looked at Flora, who chewed on her bottom lip.

"I saw Tess Thursday night, but I was not with her," he said.

"And you can't explain that at all? It's so secret. There is nothing you can tell me?" Flora asked.

"I know it will sound tired and cliché, but I cannot explain the business."

Gregory wanted to explain more, but as he tried to think of something to give her that was non-damning, a horn sounded. It shook him out of his thought process, and he watched Flora gather up her purse and walk to the door.

"You called a cab?"

"I do not deal with lies, Gregory."

"But, Flora, I—"

"You can't tell me. You have said that," she said. "And the only thing that you can tell me is that you left me, to go be with another woman. A woman who saunters over here half-dressed to have coffee with you each morning. You can do whatever you want, but I only date one person at a time. You could have been honest enough to tell me you had other friends."

Gregory met her steady gaze as she waited for him to give her something in return. The horn beeped again, and even though his brain spun in desperation, he couldn't think of anything to say. He stood stunned as she walked out the door. As it slammed shut, he ran to it and leaned against the frame. He did nothing as she gave him one final look and then got into the cab. Only after the cab rumbled back up his driveway did his brain kick in, and he started to think of the many things he could have said.

Tess was lying about the nature of our relationship. Let me explain...

I am part of a group, sort of like the Masons. Nothing illegal, but we don't share with outsiders...

I didn't call sooner because I was embarrassed I had to leave so suddenly...

Tess didn't call me on Thursday night. My friends were concerned because I have never missed a meeting before…

Any damn thing to make her stay, so he could explain. Except he couldn't explain anything to Flora. At best, it would have sounded like he was an alcoholic, but even that would not have been the truth. For the first time in years, Gregory felt the constraint of his being a werewolf and wanted to shout at the unfairness of it all.

Well, you see, Flora Blu, I am a werewolf. I found out when I was a teenager when our leader, Marcus, came and found me and my best friends acting out because we were close to shifting and didn't know what to do with all of the pent-up energy we had. Tess is a werewolf, too, so when she said we were together on Thursday, she meant for a hunt in our wolf forms. So, you see, it wasn't what you thought. I didn't sleep with her. She and I just happened to be in the same vicinity.

Gregory sat down on his couch and was rewarded as her scent rose up and greeted him. He couldn't believe that she had just left him. Everything still spun around in his head, because no matter which way he tried to look at it, it just didn't make any damn sense. In the time it had taken to get some eggs, his morning went from fantastic to horrible.

"I just went and got the damn eggs for breakfast," he muttered. "I would have never left her here alone had I imagined that Tess would have pulled such a stunt. Who does something like this? She said she was dating someone else, so why be upset when I do the same? I don't want to deal with this petty jealousy shit. Damn that woman."

He was on his feet and walking toward the door before his intentions made it to the conscious part of his brain. His steps grew more forceful and purposeful as he made quick work of the five hundred feet between their houses. Her footprints in the dew-slicked grass made his hackles rise, and he actually growled. As he walked, his ire rose at the complete violation of privacy. He saw Tess sitting on her deck and watched her posture change the moment she noticed him. She tentatively raised a hand to wave to him as he came closer but lowered it when he didn't return the wave.

"Good morning, Gregory," she said as he walked up to her.

"What did you say to her?" he thundered.

She raised her mug and took a long, deliberate drink before answering him. Whether to buy time for him or her, he wasn't certain. Their eyes met, and she put her mug down. He resisted the urge to slap it off of the deck. The last fight he started had been when he was fourteen, and he didn't want to start anything physical, especially with Tess.

"It was just general chit-chat while I made coffee," she said. "She looked completely lost as she snooped through your cupboards. I helped her."

"Tess," he rumbled. "Cut the crap. What did you say to Flora?"

"Flora? Oh, that's her name," Tess said as she stood. "I mentioned we met up Thursday night. That's all. Then I made the coffee, poured us each a mug, and left. Well, I guess I might have mentioned that we often have coffee together in the morning."

"For someone who was worried I would be upset about our fling being over, you certainly are acting like a jealous bitch."

He watched her flinch as he flung the words at her, but he wasn't done. As Tess sat back down, Gregory paced in front of her. He tried to reign in the anger before he said things he wouldn't be able to take back. The longer he paced, the more agitated her posture became. She sat back and crossed her arms.

"You set the terms for our little, winter fuck-fest, remember?" he sneered. "I didn't ask you to marry me or anything. When you said you were done, I accepted that. The whole situation was a casual one of convenience. We weren't even dating."

"But, Gregory—" she started.

"But what? You were bored and wanted to move on. Spring fever or some crap, right? I didn't stop you. I didn't beg like some love-sick puppy. You were ready to see other people, and you know what,

Tess? So was I," he said. "The biggest difference is that I would have never tried to sabotage your new relationship."

He watched Tess process the information. He took a step closer to her, her height allowing her to meet him almost eye-to-eye. The look she gave him was anything but apologetic. Tess ran a finger over his shoulder. He grabbed her hand and flung it away from him. "So, you're in a relationship with her?" she asked. "That seems awfully quick for you."

"Do not push this back at me," Gregory snapped. "You crossed the line when you went over to my home the moment you saw me leave."

"It's not like I went over with the intention of meeting your evening's entertainment," she snapped back.

"Somehow I don't believe you. She left because of the lies you told her."

"Then apparently, she doesn't know you that well. Are you sure this is the woman you want to get involved with?"

He took a step back and inhaled deeply to calm himself. Never before had he wanted to shake a person so badly in his life. Gregory resumed pacing while Tess sat back down and casually sipped her coffee. He wanted to impress upon her just how immature and wrong her actions were. Meeting her eyes, he knew just what would hit home for her.

"I hope you are happy with yourself, Tess," he said in a quiet and calm voice. "You, who pride yourself on being fair and having some sense of honor, just crapped all over what was left of the friendship we had. You deliberately lied to our friends to make them worry about me. You also lied to a woman you have never met and don't even know, because of your petty jealousy."

"I—"

Gregory held up a hand to stave off her protests and pinned her with a heated stare.

"You what? You made sure I had no choice with Flora and left me in the worst position possible. You knew I couldn't tell her about my situation. You knew I couldn't possibly explain why I had to leave so urgently. And you planted the idea that I left her to be with you. Not to mention, you violated my privacy by exposing the sordid relationship we did have."

His voice had risen with each accusation, and he watched Tess deflate and then curl into herself as shame took over.

"I want nothing to do with you outside of pack matters, Tess," he said. "Never come to my home again."

He held her gaze for a few moments more and then turned and stormed off her deck. He heard her make a few soft and feeble protests, but he didn't turn to acknowledge them. Gregory felt a grim satisfaction course through him. The one area he knew for certain that Tess would take seriously was her sense of honor. He went back into his kitchen, stared at the eggs, and began to curse a blue streak. He put the eggs in the fridge, carefully, and then grabbed a beer.

Gregory emptied half the bottle in one long pull and then slammed it on the counter. It foamed but didn't spill over. He glared at the coffee pot, snatched it up, and poured the contents down the drain. He wanted to yell and break things, but the small rational part of his brain reminded him that he would ultimately be the one to have to clean it all up.

He grabbed his phone and prayed that Flora had left him a message. Even if she was telling him to piss off, it would mean she was still open to communication. The cheerful cartoon-turtle wallpaper mocked him with the lack of notices. Gregory sighed, moved to the bedroom, and began to change the sheets.

Chapter 13

Flora stepped out of the cab and handed the driver a few bills. As she thrust a handful of cash at him, she realized she had just tipped him ten dollars and didn't care. The cab driver had earned it by not keeping up the traditional stream of chatter. It had been a blessedly quiet ride all the way home. She walked up the four flights to her home, and once she had made it inside, she shut and locked the door. Suddenly boneless, she leaned against it and let her anguish consume her. Tears slipped down her face as she stood there. She gave in to the shock and hurt and had the most, snot-bubble-blowing, mouth-trembling, sub-sub having, ugliest cry possible. While it released the emotions, she felt drained and incredibly filthy.

She looked down at her clothes, glad she had changed into them, pushed off the door, and went to take a long and cleansing shower. She wanted to scrub Gregory Bell out of her system, off her skin, and out of her mind. The heat from the water did little to relax her, and being enveloped in her favorite scent began to calm her. She scrubbed down twice more and finally shut the water off.

Stepping out of the shower, she heard her phone bleep and sighed. Flora hoped that Gregory was not the type of person to blow her phone up with texts. She needed time to think and create some sort of plan. Intellectually, she knew that it was improbable that Gregory had never been with another woman. However, she had not expected to have some strange woman come and toss around claims the morning after having had glorious sex with him. Even worse, the bitch had insinuated that Flora was a mere distraction.

"I am no one's rebound," she muttered.

Her phone bleeped again, and she sighed. She wrapped a towel around her body and walked over to where her tablet sat on her dresser. She pushed a button and spoke.

"Transfer phone texts, password 'ziggy, zee, 023573."

She put the tablet down and slowly got dressed. Flora knew she was stalling in case of an onslaught, but after her start to the morning, it was her prerogative. She picked a light, lilac-colored sundress that boasted lovely silver sequins that swirled down the bodice and over the skirt. It was cheerful and sassy, and she hoped that wearing it would bring her mood up. Squaring her shoulders, she picked up the tablet. Four texts from Shonise, none from Gregory.

"This might actually be worse," she muttered.

Flora knew she could ignore Gregory until he got the hint to go away. She was afforded no such luck with her best friend. She quickly ran through the options: 0—she could text Shonise a glowing report and buy herself a few days, or 1—she could tell her best friend the truth and indulge in the comfort that she would provide. Rather a no brainer for a programmer, so she got undressed, put on her rattiest, most comfortable pair of jammies, and then called Shonise.

"Okay, spill it, sister," Shonise greeted her.

Much to Flora's surprise, she burst into tears and squeaked when she tried to speak.

"His ex-girlfriend came to the house this morning to let me know she wasn't so much an ex," Flora said through a hiccup. "At least she made me some coffee."

A few moments of silence hung in the air.

"I will be there in ten—no, wait—a half hour. I need to get supplies," Shonise said. "Love you. Be there soon."

Flora nodded at the screen and went to find a box of Kleenex.

True to her word, Shonise showed up exactly thirty minutes later. She had two bags filled with emergency supplies that she set on the kitchen counter. Flora watched as she unpacked. Bag one held a pint of strawberry cheesecake ice cream and another of Mackinaw Island Fudge. In addition, there were two T-bone steaks, four potatoes, sour cream, greens, and thick-cut bacon. The second bag produced more goodies: six bottles of wine, margarita mix, a bottle of rum, and the ingredients of buttermilk, cherries, and chocolate chips. Shonise had planned to be there for at least two days, and Flora knew there would be mass indulgence the entire time.

Once the supplies were put away, Flora turned to face her friend. Shonise had her arms out, and Flora went into the hug and felt the tension leave as she cried again until hoarse. She finally pulled away to wipe her nose and stared at her friend. There were no more tears, so she nodded, and the two went moved from the kitchen to the living room, with their snacks in tow.

A few hours later, they sat on the couch, sharing the strawberry cheesecake ice cream. Flora waved her spoon about animatedly as she vented.

"I mean, it's not like I am in love with this guy," she snorted. "I have only known him for a few weeks at most."

"I know that's right," Shonise concurred.

"But who in the hell has their ex over for damn coffee every morning? You should have seen her, shaking her ass all the way into the house, wearing booty shorts and a tired old tank top. Looked like the run-down, ratty version of one of a booby-shirt," Flora said, digging her spoon in deep. "Even drank out of an owl cup, the skank."

"Doesn't sound much like an ex if she struts around wearing next to nothing when she visits," Shonise said.

"Right? I mean, if *he* wants to have casual sex with a person, at least be honest and tell them it's a hook-up. *He* was acting like this was the start to something," Flora said.

Shonise nodded and stabbed her spoon into the ice cream. Flora smiled at her friend as she crammed a huge mouthful in and then tried to talk.

"I meab, duth couldna tolth hith ho to wait til you left."

Flora laughed.

"I have known you long enough to have understood every word you said. Okay, enough of wasting time talking about Gregory Bell. What are we going to marathon watch?"

Thus started the negotiations for which series they could power through. Flora was glad that Shonise deferred to her. It meant they wouldn't have to watch hours of paranormal, freaky shows that would give her nightmares. Instead, they settled for watching true crime shows where women got revenge by murdering their lovers. It seemed appropriate.

The next morning, Flora woke up and stretched languidly across her bed. The fact that she had not kicked Shonise, along with the heavenly scents of bacon and coffee, meant her best friend had made breakfast. She sat up and swung her feet over the bed. She found her slippers and shuffled into the kitchen. Flora took the mug of coffee Shonise handed her and sat at the kitchen bar. She emptied the mug and held it out for a refill. She smiled as a plate stacked high with chocolate cherry chip buttermilk pancakes were slid under her nose.

"Are you sure you won't be my wife?"

Flora was semi-serious in her asking as she stuffed a huge forkful of pancakes in her mouth.

"Nuh uh, my dear. Strictly dickly here," Shonise grinned as she joined Flora at the bar. "But I will always cook my famous pancakes for my best friend when she needs me."

Flora nodded as she ate more of the goodness. The marathon watching wasn't quite over yet. The night before, they had chosen to watch scorned women who had been murderous. Today's selection was all about revenge through destruction of property. While some of the plots were laughable, a few seemed possible to Flora. Even worse, Shonise was excited about all of the possibilities.

"We could sabotage his car," Shonise said. "We could cover it with eggs and let it strip the paint."

"Do you remember what trouble we got into doing that?" Flora giggled.

When Flora and Shonise had been thirteen, they had tried to run away. Shonise knew she had gotten a D in math and had planned to run away before report cards were sent home. Flora had tried to talk her friend into tutoring sessions for months, but Shonise just knew she would be getting at least a B. After hysterical tears at seeing her grade and claims of parental abuse to come, a plan for survival was hatched. She told Flora about her plan to go to her cousin's house in Detroit to stay for a few days. Once she got settled, she would then head to

Chicago to be a fashion designer. Despite Shonise's assertions that she would be fine, there was no way Flora was going to let her best friend walk alone. Shonise had been the stronger personality in their friendship, so Flora agreed to go along with the plans.

Flora had packed a small bag with three sets of clothes. She was afraid of what could happen. The trip was almost sixty miles and would take nineteen and a half hours to walk. Despite Shonise's upbeat attitude and claims that it would be fun, Flora had some doubts. As they left school that day, they began their long walk toward their new life. She did manage to talk her friend into getting supplies from Farmer Jack's first. Being practical, Flora got bread, bologna, apples, and granola bars.

They managed to get four miles away from the school before Shonise's mother pulled up alongside them, out of her mind with fear, which she demonstrated through angry words and threats of great bodily harm. The girls got meekly into the car and listened to a lecture about their stupidity that escalated once their plan to walk to Detroit came out. The lecture continued until Flora's mother came to get her.

Flora had explained the whole situation to her mother, who in her wisdom decided that Flora had been acting like a dedicated friend. After another firm lecture, her parents tasked her to stand by her beliefs and to act on what was right, not what was easy.

"Yeah, that was something," Shonise said grimly. "I hate bologna to this day. Can you believe they were going to make me eat the whole package that night?"

"Uh huh," Flora giggled. "I can't believe it all landed on your dad's car."

Shonise had avoided her punishment by throwing each slice of bologna out of the kitchen window. The pieces of processed meat stayed on the car all night and through the next, sunny day. While the acid in the meat stripped the clear coat off the car, the real issue was the stench of rotting bologna. Shonise had been made to eat another package of bologna, in front of her parents, and the girls were grounded from sleepovers for two months.

The two laughed as they talked over each other, filling in the gory details of having to wash the car inside out and the months of math tutoring Flora insisted Shonise take from her to make sure her grades never dipped so low again. It was the moment their friendship had shifted to the girls being equal partners in their exploits. Soon, they came back to the original conversation.

"How about spraying some bear musk on him or something?" Flora asked. "He's always out in those stupid woods. It would serve him right to get mauled by a bear."

The girls laughed, and the jokes got ruder about Gregory's encounter with the bear. After the breakfast plotting, Flora had a quiet moment while she cleaned the dishes and Shonise took a shower. She appreciated that her friend had such inventive ways of expressing her outrage. Everything from coating his car in rubber cement and leaving it to bake in the sun to throwing stink bombs in the cabin window.

"I know," Shonise exclaimed.

"What?" Flora said,

"We can bleach the turtle pond."

"No, we certainly cannot do that, Shonise," she said. "That is my paying gig, remember?"

"Well, it would be easier to catalogue the shells if they were sitting still in front of you on a counter," Shonise reasoned.

"No. Those poor turtles can't help that they are in the same vicinity as that ass hat," Flora grumbled. "We will not be destroying the pond."

She walked back into the living room and settled on the couch to watch more vengeful women. After an episode where the woman dissolved her cheating husband in a vat of industrial acid, Flora was done.

"Okay, I have got to do something else," she said. "I can't just sit in my apartment forever."

"Please do not drag me to one of your dance class, workout things," Shonise moaned. "I mean, if we are going to do some dancing, can't we do hip-hop or something I know how to do?"

"Look, this dance system has been around for like a decade. It's fun and a good workout. Come on."

Flora took the eye-rolling as consent and went to her room to change. An hour later, both women dragged themselves out of the gym, hair slicked with sweat.

"I cannot believe you made me do that," Shonise said.

"It's good for you."

"No. A margarita is good for me. This working out thing makes me hurt."

Flora laughed.

"Fine. Let's go change and go out for lunch. I will buy you at least one huge margarita."

It took almost three hours and two margaritas for Shonise to forgive her. As they made plans to visit the bookstore in Holly and perhaps sneak away for a road trip, Flora relaxed. Unlike the last time, it would not take her months to get over this guy. As they slowly walked back to Flora's apartment, a realization hit her. She felt sick to her stomach and took a deep breath to calm herself. As she looked at the concerned face of her friend, she knew what she needed to do.

"Shonise! I need a huge favor," Flora said. "This is big time."

Chapter 14

Gregory had woken early and forced himself to clean his home so he wouldn't show up to work hours early and have to sit and wait for Flora. She had not answered his texts or calls for four days. In his desperation, he had not even been subtle when asking Ginny what time Flora came in on Wednesdays. If nothing else, he knew Flora loved her schedules. For weeks, she had come by at the same time each day to collect her pictures and data. Of course, she had altered the schedule after their last encounter. He knew it might be stalkerish and probably cross some line of potential harassment, but today he planned on having a talk with her.

He waited up in the observation post and tried to work on a report that was due later that week. He made some notes and pretended he wasn't looking up at every rustle of brush. Finally disgusted and slightly amused with his teenage behavior, Gregory had given in and actually was filling out the report when a wide, tan hat came into his view. He wanted to rush down and scoop her up but knew that was a stupid plan. Instead, he waited for her to collect data from at least half of the cameras.

Gregory carefully and quietly walked down from the outpost. He made it around the pond with superb timing as Flora bent over to collect from the last camera. He drank in the sight of her lime green sundress that matched her black and green galoshes. As he got closer, he saw the green blobs on her boots were actually turtles. He smiled and tried to act casual.

"Did you get good pictures today?"

He winced when she shrieked, but he smoothly caught her as she pitched and fell toward the water. Gregory pulled her in close and almost dropped her from shock.

"You're not Flora," he said.

The light brown eyes went from wide in shock to narrow in irritation and stabbed daggers through his face.

"You're touching me."

Being run over would have felt better than the words flung at him. Gregory quickly set the woman on her feet and backed up to give her space. No doubt she knew who he was, which clearly made her a friend of Flora's. His good mood plummeted.

"I'm sorry to have startled you. I expected someone else."

"Obviously. This is why she sent me out to get these damn turtle pictures."

The heat from her glare was nothing compared to the once-over she dismissed him with.

"I'm Gregory," he said and extended his hand.

"Shonise."

She looked at his hand as if he had just wiped his ass and stuck it out for her. Her eyes crawled up from his hand to his arm and then up to meet his eyes, withering everything along the way. He withdrew his hand before she could chew it off. He stood a few more moments in silence and then cleared his throat.

"Is Flora okay?" he asked.

The tilt of her head and rolling eyes was his answer.

"I need to explain some things to her," he started.

"Actually, I will explain some things to you," Shonise interrupted, her voice going quiet. "I'll be sure to use tiny words so you can understand me."

While Gregory could appreciate Shonise's loyalty to Flora, he felt like a mouse being stalked. Whether by raptor or viper, he wasn't sure. The only thing he knew was that this was going to be uncomfortable, and she would strike when he least expected it.

"A few years ago, Flora met this guy. He came in and swept her off her feet, made her giddy and giggly, like you have. He was her first real boyfriend, and she fell hard. While Flora worked and went to school, this jerk sat at home. Standard story of crap that he was looking for a job and this and that. Instead, he spent his time in an online game," Shonise said. "And while she worked and planned a future together, he cheated on her. When she found out, it broke her spirit."

"What a load of crap. He sounds like a prick," Gregory said and received a look that dared him to talk again before the telling was done.

"It was crap, as you so articulately put it. What you don't understand is that Flora is all binary—0's and 1's. You are either off or on with her, and because of her last experience, there is no going back for her. Once you break her trust, you might as well disappear."

Gregory met the heated stare from Shonise and nodded.

"I like her a lot," he said after a few moments. "It was all a misunderstanding, and I did a bad job of explaining."

"Poor job," Shonise said.

"Right, that's what I said."

"No, *you* used incorrect grammar."

Gregory took a breath and tried not to yell at his only hope for getting Flora back. He watched Shonise tap on the tablet a few more times and tried to figure out what he could say to her. Before he could get any more out, she turned to face him again.

"Just understand one thing, Gregory," she said.

"What is that?"

"You are already a zero. She's done with you."

She picked up a small tote and walked away from him.

Taking a deep breath, he pulled his phone from his back pocket and made a call.

"Marcus, I really need to talk with you."

Gregory paced in anticipation of everything going to crap. After his phone call to Marcus, he had been made to wait until the following Monday before having their meeting. Marcus had taken his daughter to Ann Arbor for a science camp at the university, and the weekend had been the showcase of their inventions. All of which meant Gregory had to replay the ugly scenes with Flora, Tess, and to top it off, Shonise many, many times in his head. He also got to think about the wonderful night he had spent with Flora and the morning after. There was no separating the events, because everything had happened within twenty-four hours. And then he replayed the words with Tess, which still pissed him off. He never expected her to play dirty for no reason. She had moved on before him. His phone rang, and for a split second he had hope. But then he looked at the display and sighed.

"Hey, Mathias," he said.

Gregory impatiently listened to his friend for almost ten minutes. There was a lot of talk about stars, nature, and a possible collaboration of their programs. He did a lot of grunting and non-verbal replies. At some point, he became aware that Mathias had paused. He was thankful his friend knew him well enough not to pry too deeply.

"Yes, I am still here. Sorry. I'm a bit preoccupied."

Gregory didn't get mad at the laughter, but instead used it as a quick excuse to hang up the phone. He walked outside and then back in. He tied up the trash bag and walked it down his driveway to the can for collection. He came back in, replaced the bag, and when he looked at his watch one more time, a whole three minutes had passed.

"Are you kidding me?"

His meeting was at seven o'clock that night and it was currently six-forty-five. The fifteen minutes might as well have been a lifetime. Marcus lived only three cabins down to the right, which would take all of three minutes to walk, so Gregory needed to occupy himself for the next seven minutes. He looked around his cabin and decided to straighten his living room. He put the two videos on the coffee table back in their cases and away in the tower. He pushed the recliner back a few inches for better television viewing. He moved the cushions on the couch and was rewarded with a puff of air that contained Flora's perfume.

"Dammit," he muttered.

Gregory grabbed his phone and started to send Flora another text. So far, he had started eight drafts but had never finished any of them. Part of the delay was waiting on Marcus's answer, and the other half was delaying any rejection she might have for him. He put his phone back in his pocket and sighed. There was no point in starting a conversation where he wouldn't be able to answer any questions. He just wanted it to be over. He looked at his watch, and finally it was time to go.

And then he dragged his feet the whole time, walking the scant few yards separating his home from Marcus's. He saw Marcus inside, moving from the kitchen to the living room. A shadowed wave from the font window meant he had been spotted as well. Gregory picked up his pace. He knocked on the door to buy just a few more seconds.

"It's serious, then," Marcus said, opening the door. "You haven't knocked on my door since you were thirteen."

"There is a bit of a mess," Gregory started and then paused.

Marcus waved him into the living room and motioned for him to sit. Marcus walked to the kitchen and returned with a couple of beers and two plates.

"Given your tone on the phone, I figured we were going to need some food."

Gregory smiled. It was the little gestures that made Marcus the great leader, friend, and man that he was. He placed a plate of fried fish and a garden mix of vegetables on the coffee table.

"I know you're grown, but as long as you are my guest..." Marcus started.

"I will happily eat the vegetables," Gregory chuckled. "Yes, even the mushrooms that you tried to hide under the red peppers and broccoli. I haven't tried to get out of eating vegetables for years now."

"Has it really been that long since we had a meal together?"

"It's been a minute since we've had a meal and a private conversation," Gregory said. "I just now realized how much I miss it."

"Good thing about you becoming Alpha is that we will have many more dinners to come," Marcus said. "Of course, you already know you are welcome."

He sat back and enjoyed the light dinner and easy conversation. While Gregory really wanted to ask his question, he knew Marcus would start that conversation when he was ready, which wouldn't be until after dinner. The ploy was not new. Ever since Marcus had become his mentor, there was always a period of quiet and easy conversation before anything serious would be discussed. After a decadent dessert had been eaten, it was time.

"What is on your mind, Gregory?"

"An issue has risen, and I need to talk to you," Gregory started. "Because I think I am going to need to make a major step."

"What happened?"

Keeping to the facts, Gregory explained to Marcus his budding relationship with Flora and then the altercation with Tess. He tried to stay true to the details and keep the bitterness out of his voice. He had played the scenes over in his mind through the whole weekend; the accusations from Flora, the tension, and all the desperation he had gone through from Tess's careless words. While the incident still made him fume, what he was asking for was not about relationship advice.

"I want to tell Flora the truth about me."

"You know what happens if she doesn't come on board?"

"Yes, but it will work out fine," Gregory said.

Gregory resisted the urge to run all the way to work. Having Marcus's approval to open up to Flora and give her the chance to learn everything felt like he had been given a boon. He had a new hope, but it did depend on getting help. As he approached the pond, he saw the familiar tan hat and actually smiled.

"Hi, Shonise," he greeted.

He was nice and loud to avoid sneaking up on her again. She shrieked, dropped her tote, and gave him a baleful glare.

"What the hell, Gregory? I am not deaf. You certainly didn't need to shout like that."

"My apologies," he said. "I was just trying not to sneak up on you."

Shonise stared at him pointedly.

"Why are you here?" she asked.

"I don't want to be a zero," he said and then shook his head. "That sounded better in my head."

"I already told you," Shonise said. "Flora doesn't take chances anymore."

"But I know I can be her One," Gregory said.

"Then explain Thursday night," Shonise said.

Gregory looked her in the eye and held her gaze.

"I was at a meeting," he said.

"One that you couldn't talk to Flora about?" she sneered. "Are you in a gang or something?"

"One that requires anonymity for the safety of the members," he said.

He watched Shonise's face as her eyes grew wider and sudden understanding lit her eyes. He would forever be grateful to Marcus for the suggestion to stay ambiguous with the information and let Shonise draw her own conclusions.

"Oh, a twelve-step," she said. "But that doesn't explain all the texts and calls she said you got. Those meetings are voluntary."

"Not when another member needs to reach you," he said carefully.

"What happened that you couldn't tell her? Was it your sponsor?"

"No, it was Nathaniel," he said as he shoved his friend under the bus with no regrets. "I sponsor him, and he really needed me that night. I didn't tell Flora because I was a bit rattled. I thought something was wrong, with all the calls I was getting. We were just getting to know each other, and I hadn't found the right time to talk to her about the meetings or my group."

Shonise nodded in understanding. He watched her work through the new information and hoped she would take it. She nodded to herself a few times, narrowed her eyes as she processed other information, and then gave him a curious look.

"Why did you tell me all of this instead of telling her?" she asked.

Gregory didn't like the suspicious look on her face.

"I can't just show up at her place, else I get arrested for harassment," he said. "And this isn't the kind of information you just dump into a text. I want to tell her everything face-to-face. It was badly handled."

"Why? You all have known each other six weeks. It's not like you are madly in love."

"I beg to differ," Gregory said. "Flora might think she operates in binary, but that is not the sexy, giggly, nature-hating woman I met. She is wonderfully complex, intelligent, and so willing to go off on adventures. I know there is more to this relationship we have, because she came on a nature walk with me. So, she really likes me. And I do love her. When I think about losing her, I get sick. I would quit my job and move into the city if it meant keeping her happy. I just need a chance."

"So what are you going to do?" Shonise asked.

"This is where I need your help," Gregory said. "I need you to convince her to talk to me, or at the very least, hear me out."

"Wait a minute," Shonise said.

Gregory didn't like the sour look covering her face again.

"Yes?"

"We planned a menu that included wine, and Flora told me about the wine you brought as a gift."

"It was a gift for her," he said. "I've learned to control myself."

He mentally sighed as he realized he would never be able to have a drink around Shonise, ever. As she was Flora's best friend, he figured the number of dinners and casual gatherings would be high, and he again sighed. Being around Shonise made him want a drink.

"Oh, okay. That says a lot about you."

Shonise opened the tote and grabbed the tablet. She tapped away and after a few moments looked up at him.

"What about your ex who came over for coffee?"

"Tess was being petty from her jealousy. I made it clear to her to stay away from me," Gregory said. "That wasn't something I could have anticipated, because to my knowledge, it was all over. I believed her when she said she was good with our breakup."

Shonise grunted and tapped more on the tablet. Gregory stood and waited. After four minutes, Shonise looked up at him.

"I will help you. Be at her place tonight at seven. I will meet you at the entry door, and she will at least listen to you."

"Thank you," Gregory said and then noticed an odd object in the tote bag. "Is that bleach?"

"Yes."

"You can't clean the instruments with bleach. It will make the turtles sick," he said.

"It wasn't going to be used to clean the instruments. If you had turned out to be an asshole, I would have had to bleach the pond."

Shonise bent her head toward the tablet and tapped away some more. Gregory tried to make eye contact to see if she was joking. He met her eyes. She wasn't. He left her in peace to finish her work, slightly horrified.

"I wonder if she's actually one of us," he muttered as he walked back to the visitor's center. "She's scary enough to be."

Chapter 15

Flora scrubbed her face with the bottom of her shirt. As she lifted her head, a bead of missed sweat dripped into her left eye with a burning intensity. She cursed the headband she wore for failing at its one job. She rubbed her eye as she moved faster and pushed herself harder. Moving didn't make her eye feel any better, but it kept her attention. The loud, throbbing music of her dance workout did nothing to erase the conversation she had had with Shonise that morning.

"I'm done getting your turtle pictures. Put on your big-girl pants and go do your job. I have to get my classes ready."

And just like that, Flora was back on the schedule to visit For-Mar. She was so upset that, even though she had already done her workout earlier in the morning, she decided an evening class would burn up the stress and allow her to get a good night's sleep before having to confront Gregory. She danced and kicked her legs higher and as hard as she could. Her thighs burned, and at one point she wanted to just stop moving, but the thought of having to look into Gregory's eyes made her move despite the exhaustion. The sudden quiet meant her hour of stress release was done, and she dried her face with a towel. She said good night to the people she worked out with and made it back to her apartment before the last of her energy failed her. Shonise standing in front of her door was a surprise and put her on alert. There had been no text or phone call.

"Why are you here?" she asked. "Is something wrong? Did someone die?"

"Calm down, Flora. No one died," Shonise said with a smile.

"Why are you here?" Flora grumbled at her. "You are the reason I had to do an extra work out class today. I am all stressed out about having to watch out for that man tomorrow."

"Well, since you didn't add me to your company payroll, I thought you should have to do your own work," Shonise said. "Unless you *are* going to pay me? Or, hey, set up my classroom…"

Flora rolled her eyes at her best friend but felt like something was off. She knew Shonise too well and could tell there was more to the visit.

"I can pay you."

"Okay, offer rescinded. This is not the end of the world," Shonise said. "Go finish your turtle project."

"You know why I asked you to step in," Flora started.

"Yes, I do," Shonise said.

Flora got a chill from the look her friend gave her.

"What did you do?" she squeaked out.

"I listened," Shonise said and walked to the stairwell door.

Flora watched Gregory emerge and shot Shonise a murderous look. When that got no reaction, she tried for pleading panic, which her friend still ignored. She tensed when pulled into a tight hug from her friend.

"Worst friend ever," Flora whispered.

"Just listen to him," Shonise said. "I wouldn't have set this up if it didn't sound legit."

And with that, her friend released her and walked through the stairwell door, leaving her with unwanted company. Flora drew in a deep breath and turned to stare at Gregory, who still said nothing. She thought about walking into her home and closing the door, but it wouldn't solve anything, so she stared back. After the buzzing of the safety lights made her head hurt, she gave in.

"Okay. You have one minute to explain," she demanded.

"Fair enough. Can we go into your apartment?" Gregory asked.

The rich sound of his voice made her stomach flutter and warmth spread through her body. She wasn't at all happy with the traitorous reaction to hearing him speak. She stared at him and crossed her arms over her chest.

"Why?"

"Because I would like some privacy, and there is none in this hallway. Shonise knows I am here," he said and grinned. "I expect her to call in about fifteen minutes and come to your rescue if you don't answer."

Flora had to nod in agreement, because it was accurate. She wanted to be furious at him, but just seeing him made her want to be in his embrace. Still, she pushed those feeling back and feigned indifference. She walked into her home and let him follow. Once the door shut, Flora turned to face him.

"Why did you leave me on Thursday?"

"I didn't have a choice, and I couldn't tell you the truth. It's rather hard to understand."

"How about you try to explain?" she asked.

"I ask that you keep an open mind."

"I will try my best. You have fifty seconds," she said.

"You wanted to know where I was on Thursday."

"Right, since Tess made it sound like you were with her and you had no decent answer."

"I was near her, as in we were in the same vicinity, but I wasn't with her. I had to go for a run that night, and she made my friends worry about me. So, they blew up my phone until I answered," he said.

"That explains not a damn thing," Flora huffed. "You seriously left what we were doing to go on a run? Thirty seconds."

"I'm a werewolf," Gregory said.

Flora blinked at him, not sure she had just heard him correctly. She searched his face for some hint that he might be trying to diffuse the situation with a joke. There was none.

"What?"

"I am a werewolf," he said. "I'm not sure how or why, but I found out when I was a teen. I have to shift into my wolf form each night of the full moon every month. My pack gets together and goes for a run. Safety in numbers and everything."

"That is the worst lie I have ever heard," Flora said. "Werewolves aren't real."

"Actually, we are, but we stay hidden because it is dangerous to be different in this world. It's hard enough being a man of color, let alone a paranormal man of color."

"One of us is suffering from some kind of delusion," she scoffed.

"Flora, out of the millions of things I could say to you, why would I claim to be a werewolf? I could have given you the same story I gave Shonise," he said. "I just didn't figure lying to you was an option. So, I went with the truth."

"I am going to need some pretty awesome proof of this."

Before she knew it, Gregory had started to unbutton his shirt. Flora pulled a Taser from her purse and held it up as warning.

"Just what the hell do you think you are doing?" she asked.

To her surprise, Gregory chuckled.

"Since there is a full moon tonight, I am going to shift and show you. You need proof, and I have no other way to prove what I say is real. Not to mention, I really like this shirt and don't want to rip it up, so I am taking it off. I won't make any moves towards you. Just don't scream. Please," he said and then pretended to be shocked. "I can't believe you just threatened to taze me."

"Only if you are lying about this whole werewolf thing and are taking your shirt off for...some other reason," she said, happy her voice wasn't shaking. "I swear, I will shock you into unconsciousness if you try anything nefarious."

"Flora Blu, you asked for proof," he said gently. "I am just going to shift between forms to prove to you that I am not lying. Once I shift, there should be no doubt I am telling you the truth."

Flora nodded, her lips pressed tight, forcing herself not to enjoy the way he always said her name. She watched in silence as Gregory finished taking off his clothes, folded them neatly, and stood naked in her foyer. Then a loud pop sounded, and his body seemed to fold in on itself. She watched with rapt attention as he shrunk down and fur grew in long strands all over him. Within just a few seconds, Gregory the man was gone and a rather large, gray wolf stood before her. Her hands shook and clenched. Flora watched the wires and probes from her Taser strike the wolf, and it fell to the ground with a yelp. She released the wires from her unit. After the wolf stopped twitching, she quickly pulled the probes out of his heaving side. The fur was warm, and she could feel his rapid heartbeat. She patted him a few times and then sighed.

"I guess you are telling the truth," she said. "I wonder how we are going to work with this twist. I really don't like nature. And apparently you are all about the nature."

She scuttled backwards when his bones started to pop and shift again. Soon, there was a naked man on her foyer floor. His caramel eyes sought hers, and he scowled.

"What was that? You said…if I wasn't telling…the truth," he gasped out.

"I panicked," she said and then burst into semi-hysterical laughter. "Do you shed? I really don't want a boyfriend who sheds. Oh my goodness, you really are a werewolf. I should have bought the other book.

She laughed while he picked himself up off the floor and got dressed. Flora finally had it under control by the time he stood before her. A few moments of a silent but not hostile stare-off gave her time to collect herself.

"Well then, I guess you proved your story. Nature seriously has it out for me," she said, then wrinkled her brow. "How did you convince Shonise?

"Oh, I allowed her to think I had a twelve-step meeting to go to," he grinned. "It was easier than trying to get naked in front of her."

Flora burst back into laughter and shook her head.

"So, do you believe me?"

"How can I not? The evidence was pretty amazing," she said. "Hey, why aren't you still affected by the electro-shock?"

"Oh, that is still with the wolf form. When I shift back, it will hurt for a while," Gregory said and shuddered.

"Pain is tied with each form? That could be really useful," Flora mused.

"Yes, injuries tend to stay with the form it was received in. Which is why I think we have survived for so long," he said. "Trust me, there is more I don't know about being a werewolf, than I do about being one."

Flora waved him toward the living room. She grabbed two glasses and poured wine for both of them. She joined him on the couch and looked at him.

"We might both need this, despite your proclivity for the drink," she said with a wink. "What do you call yourselves?"

"Werewolves."

"How long have there been werewolves?"

"Our kind has been around for millennia," he said after a good, healthy drink. "I found out when I was fourteen, along with my friends. Luckily, Marcus our Alpha, found us all and helped us transition. He was shocked to find four of us all together."

Flora nodded, digesting the information. Or at least tried to. The undeniable proof sat next to her. She half paid attention as Gregory explained his life and habits as a werewolf, including the monthly run. She interrupted him when a thought puzzled her.

"Gregory, your people have been around for millennia, and the best name you came up with was werewolf?"

She watched his caramel eyes grow wide, and he laughed. She allowed herself to be pulled into a hug.

"No, darling, but our true name can't be pronounced by the human tongue."

Flora's cheeks heated with embarrassment. Partially from digesting the information, but in honesty she reacted from being so close to him again. She didn't fight against it and snuggled closer in to him. Somewhere, her brain still spun with the information he gave her.

"So, Marcus and his family line have made it their goal to find young werewolves and rescue them?" she asked. "And now you are going to be doing the same thing?"

"Yes. Marcus wants to retire in a decade or so, and his daughter isn't one of us," Gregory said.

"So you're all born and not cursed?"

"No thanks to Hollywood for that misinformation."

"And the were-genetic doesn't breed true each generation?"

"Not to our knowledge," Gregory said. "Despite the media portrayals, the group we have is voluntary not blood bound. We are all lone wolves, who happened to be found and gathered as a pack. I'm not sure how others do it, but this is what works for us. We're very private, and that has kept us safe so far."

Flora sat back and looked up at him.

"Is it okay that you told me?"

"Yes, I got permission to do so," he said.

Flora nodded.

"I'm dating a werewolf."

"And I'm dating a human," Gregory said with a grin. "Just think, both of us are kind of different three days a month."

Flora burst into laughter.

"Wow, you really went there."

"Yeah, this is probably the only time I ever could have," he said.

They settled back into an easy silence, Flora enjoying being held by him as she turned over the improbable facts that now were the new reality in her life.

"Will you need to run tonight?" she asked suddenly.

"No, I'm pretty sure that Taser shock wore off the need to shift again."

"Did it really hurt?"

"You heard me cry out," he said.

"You kind of yelped. Or were you actually saying words?" asked. "Do you understand my words in wolf form, then?"

"Sort of. It's the whole problem of really being able to make human word with that mouth," Gregory said. "I suppose the next time I shift I can try to talk to you."

"You plan to shift around me? Why would you do that?"

"Well since you know, I can invite you to the monthly event," he said. "Not that you have to run with us, but we often have a bonfire and some beer afterwards."

"And you convinced Shonise you were a drunk and had to leave why?"

"Oh, I shoved my friend Nathaniel under the bus," he said and began to laugh. "I said I was his sponsor and had to leave."

"Poor Nathaniel," Flora said.

"Not really. He is a jerk when it comes to women."

She burst into laughter, which led Gregory to tell her about some of the antics he and his friends had indulged in. Flora got a new insight, not only into Gregory as a man, but also what kind of friend he was. She put a hand on his chest, gasping for air as he told her about the foursome and their foray into Marcus's yard after being told they were werewolves.

"You really tried to sneak up on the Alpha wolf and scare him?" she giggled. "How could you possibly have thought that would be a good idea?"

"We were fifteen, not quite the paragons of good ideas and intelligence," Gregory said. "Turns out, it was the best thing we could have done. Marcus scared some good sense into us that night. Well, most of us. 'Thaniel still is an ass from time to time."

Flora stood to refill their wine glasses. As she walked back toward him, she felt a warm glow. Once she had snuggled back into his embrace, she looked up at him. She forced herself to meet his eyes and smiled at him.

"I am glad you told me," Flora said in all seriousness. "I can work with information. It might be rough, but I can deal with the truth."

"The truth is that I was broken to think I had lost you, Flora. I'm glad you gave me a chance."

"You had Shonise on your side. I knew there must have been something special about you because she would rather ride the hate train than trust a guy."

"That sounds like a story."

"Not for tonight," she said. "I would rather spend the time getting to know you better."

She cuddled closer to him and enjoyed the rest of the evening spent in quiet talk.

Chapter 16

Gregory woke up early. He stretched and relaxed for the first time in days. His evening spent with Flora had been amazing—tazing aside. He had expected many more questions, but once she had seen the truth, she just accepted it. His mind wandered as he mused about what their future might hold, until his alarm rang and forced him to get up. He sat up, grabbed his phone, and silenced the noise. A grin covered his face as he typed out a message.

G: Good morning, beautiful.

F: Good morning.

G: What are your plans for the day?

F: I have to finish the e-store and a website. I also have this tiny, little turtle project to finish up.

G: Sounds like a busy day. Will you get a break? I kinda wanted to see you.

F: You're only saying that because I'm naked right now.

Gregory stared at his phone a few moments while her simple phrase threw his imagination into overdrive.

G: That was not fair, giving me all those lovely mind pictures before I have to get ready for work.

F: You could always take care of it.

Again, he stared at his phone. Sure, there had been kissing last night, but he figured their relationship was back at beginner's status and expected it to move slowly until Flora was comfortable again. His phone chirped, drawing his eyes to the screen.

F: Unless you already have a hand on it, which is why it is taking so long for you to answer me.

G: I would rather have your hands helping me. They are much softer than mine.

F: And my mouth is softer yet.

At that point, Gregory knew he needed to put the brakes on their conversation and get ready. Her apartment was only a twenty minute ride from his home. He was almost tempted to call in to work. He never took sick days so he had plenty of time. Instead he took a deep breath.

G: You are a feisty little tease! I have to get up and get ready for work.

F: You aren't up already?

G: Stop it.

F: Stop answering me.

G: Goodbye, Flora Blu.

He locked his phone so he wouldn't be tempted to peek at the screen and made his way to the bathroom. His shower was cold, and it still didn't help. His mind provided plenty of pictures, and he finally gave in to the temptation because there was no other way to relieve his throbbing erection. Gregory pressed his forehead against the wall and sighed. He wanted to spend every moment with Flora. He finally dried off and got dressed because his stomach demanded food. Gregory walked down to the henhouse and smiled over remembered snippets of conversations, when the cage surrounding the yard opened. He turned and met Tess's eyes, and his face took on a cool facade. He cradled his eggs carefully in his hand and walked past her.

"Nothing, then? You can't even be civil?"

Rather than turn and give in to the urge to be an ass, he walked toward his home at an unhurried pace. He also fought turning back to glare at her a few times. His life was back on track with Flora, and he wasn't going to jeopardize that by getting into a useless spat with Tess.

After his uneventful breakfast, he rode into For-Mar and got ready for his day. The first good surprise was that the Turtle Mobile was fixed and ready to go back out on the road. Since Gregory hadn't expected it back for another week, he was glad he would be able to make the trip to the Linden Park. It was hard not to appreciate the joy and excitement that spilled out of the kids. His second surprise was left in his mailbox. A simple, folded note: *Meet me at 1:30 for lunch.*

Gregory didn't even mind that Ginny smirked at him as he walked out of the employee room. He gave her a slight nod and went out to meet his first tour of the day.

"Holy balls, what did they do to you?" Ginny asked.

Gregory looked at her and shook his head.

"They were fourteen-year-old girls," he said. "The ring leader decided I was cute, and the gaggle of them spent the entire hike trying to impress me."

He made a rude face at Ginny as she laughed openly at his experience. He rolled his eyes as he answered the phone, because she was still cracking up. He made the reservation for a couple to view the Arboretum and pointedly assigned Ginny the task.

"That was just mean," she said, instantly sobering.

"Yeah," he drawled. "It was. Gotta go. I have a lunch date."

He walked out of the center before she could ply him with a million questions. Gregory walked back out to the pond and up to the outpost. It stood empty, and he looked around in confusion. It made no sense to him that Flora wouldn't be there. It was one-thirty on the dot, and she wasn't the type to be late. As he looked around, he noticed a sticky note on the door frame.

Not here, silly. Let's make a new, purple memory.

He grinned and quickly made his way toward the Lilac Path. He found her halfway down the walk, holding a picnic basket. His stomach flipped as her eyes lit up and she smiled at him.

"Hi, Gregory."

He tried to slow down a bit so it wouldn't look like he was running to her. He gave up after about a second, because he did want to run to her.

"You are braving the Lilac Path again?"

"Yeah, I figured Nature owed me a big one," she said with a grin.

"Why is that?"

"I didn't let Shonise bleach the turtle pond."

Gregory pulled Flora into a hug.

"Yes, I do think you are owed a relaxing picnic for that one," he said.

He followed her back and watched as she set up. Along with the blanket and food, Flora set out a small set of black boxes.

"Flora Blu, you do know that ultrasonic repellers don't work?" he asked in a gentle tease.

"Especially if they are MP3 speakers," she said loftily.

"Right, then. I'll shut up and let you finish your preparations."

He wisely held his tongue when she brought out candles and saved himself from another mocking when she brought out lanterns to set them in. Gregory smiled and mentally shook his head. The woman liked her ambiance. A few moments more and she looked up at him and smiled.

"Let's have lunch," she said.

Gregory sat on the blanket and accepted a glass of lemonade.

"I have to apologize," Flora said. "I really should have heard you out."

"Shonise explained your last experience," he said. "With Tess acting a fool, I can understand why you felt betrayed. Not to mention, I didn't have permission to tell you then. It all worked out for the best.

They fell into an easy conversation and enjoyed the light lunch Flora had brought. Nature behaved perfectly well; a slightly cloudy sky and a light breeze kept it from being too hot, and no rain, bugs, or birds intruded on them. Flora told him about her three new business prospects, and he smiled at her enthusiasm. He leaned back and rested on his forearms as she chatted, until a chime sounded.

"Okay, I've got to go," Flora said. "You have a tour group in twenty minutes, and I have a conference call in forty."

"Keeping track of my schedule?" he teased.

"How else was I supposed to plan this lunch?" Flora asked.

He stood and stretched, then offered her a hand. She put the basket handles into his palm and stood. Gregory walked by her side and caught her giving him sideways glances.

"Yes, Flora Blu?"

She turned her head to face him and wrinkled her nose.

"Why do you call me by my full name?"

"It rolls off my tongue," he said.

They walked to the parking lot, holding hands but saying nothing. When Gregory turned to give Flora a goodbye kiss, he watched a bevy of emotions pass over her face.

"What else is going through that busy mind of yours?"

"I think I should meet Marcus," she said.

Gregory schooled his face to not betray his surprise. He had spent most of the night trying to figure out how to tell Flora that she would have to meet his Alpha, and here she just requested it. Part of being able to tell her the truth included her becoming an honorary part of the pack. There were plenty of members who refused to tell the people in their lives the truth. But for those who wanted to tell their family, the rule was all out or all in. He didn't look forward to the lashing he would get when Flora found out those rules, but lucky for him she had already accepted the truth.

"Okay. I will make it happen, then," he said. "This is the last night of the full moon, so we have a meeting tonight, anyhow."

He leaned in and gave her a kiss goodbye, then watched as she drove down the winding drive. He smiled and shook his head at the constant surprises she brought to him. His phone chirped.

F: So, which were softer? My hands or my mouth.

G: Are you really texting and driving?

F: No. I am stopped at the stop sign. Not to mention talk-to-text is configured in my car. So, what is my softest body part?

G: I guess I will have to run a comparison test tonight. Be ready at six tonight.

F: But you have to run.

After the teasing from the morning, he decided to give as good as he got.

G: You're right. How could I have forgotten about that?

F: No need to be sarcastic.

G: True enough. Make it nine. I don't mind eating late.

F: What are you going to be eating?

G: You.

Gregory grinned, turned his phone on silent, and put it in his pocket.

Gregory pressed the door buzzer and waited. He felt amazing from a great run and the anticipation of an even better night. His run with his friends had been a fast-paced hunt as a doe and her three fawns gave them a good chase. They had probably scared the deer into old age but left them unscathed. He had made time for one beer with his friends to tell them about Flora, which ended in having to promise that they would meet her soon.

Flora was waiting in her door frame, glowing with excitement.

"I have a phone interview about a job offer from the National Zoo in D.C. to create a turtle database," she exclaimed.

Gregory allowed himself to be pulled into a kiss that put a new fire in his veins as she pressed into him. He ran his hands down her back and returned her passion. He pulled back and smiled at her as his stomach rumbled loudly.

"So, you are hungry for food after all," she grinned.

"Yeah, a twenty-mile run will do that to you," he said.

He followed her into the apartment and noticed the table was already set. The candles flickered, and by each glass of water, sat a covered plate.

"You're keeping me off the bandwagon?" he teased.

"I am happy to serve you grape juice, but I figured you will get sick of it soon enough," she said with a wink.

Gregory followed her lead and sat. As he lifted the plate cover, the scent of a well grilled steak made his mouth water. He focused on taking his time to eat the lovely meal she had prepared. Dinner went by quickly enough, and as they sat on the couch having a quiet conversation, he marveled at how multi-layered she was. He answered her many questions about his run and how it felt to run as a wolf. He put his wine glass on the table in front of them and sat back to look at her.

"Did you get enough information, Flora Blu?"

"Yes, Gregory Bell," she said and then laughed. "Well, that didn't quite roll off my tongue like I expected it to."

He leaned in and placed tiny little kisses along her mouth. Gregory moved closer as he pressed his lips against hers in a consuming kiss. His tongue mated with hers, and he ran his fingers down her shoulders and then back up. He broke the kiss and nipped down the side of her neck. At the hollow of her throat, he nipped her and then soothed the mark with his tongue. She inhaled a sharp breath but wound her arms around his neck to draw him closer.

"Gregory," she said in a husky voice.

"Yes, Flora Blu?"

He held his breath as she pushed him back and stood up. Maybe she was going to take it slower.

"Are you full?"

He was certain he would die if she stopped making out with him to offer him some dessert.

"Why do you ask?"

She unzipped the back of her dress and let it drop to the floor. Gregory feasted on the sight of her naked before him. Her nipples had tightened in the cool of the apartment, and he ached to taste them. He sat up straight and met her gaze.

"Just making sure you had room for dessert."

The simple statement along with the sight of her tongue tracing her lower lip made thinking damn near impossible as blood rushed toward more important areas.

Gregory stood up and began to kiss her again. His hands brushed down her shoulders, over her stomach and hips. He broke the kiss and began to kiss down the side of her neck. He gave quick, tiny kisses over her collarbone and up the other side. He felt her fingers tug at his shirt, and he pressed his lips to hers and kissed her until she groaned into his mouth.

He guided her gently back to the couch and smiled as she sat back. He pulled off his shirt and tossed it at her. He loved the sound of Flora's laughter and knelt beside the couch. He softly began to rub the bottom of her foot and enjoyed the slight shiver coursing through her body. He massaged her foot and slowly began to work his way up her leg. As he got to the knee, he leaned in and kissed a trail up her inner thigh.

Gregory felt her hands rest on his shoulder as he kissed and teased his way up her leg. He stopped and winked at her. Slight confusion covered her face, but it was replaced as he took her other foot and gave it a good massage as well. He spent careful time working up to her knee and began his teasing routine up her other thigh. Her breath was raspy and erratic until he reached her core. One smooth swipe of his tongue made her breathing hitch, and the sound turned him on even more. He loved how Flora reacted to his touches. As he teased and excited her, she became more vocal, and he skillfully brought her to screaming. Her hands gripped his shoulders in a vice grip, and he continued his ministrations as she moved in uncontrolled shudders. He kept a gentle pressure on her thighs to keep them open as he carried out the promise made earlier in the day.

After a final release he was certain the entire building heard with clarity, Gregory sat back and smiled at Flora. He began to run his hands up her trembling legs. His fingers traced patterns over her stomach until they reached her breasts. He leaned in and slowly took her nipple into his mouth and used his tongue to tease it as his fingers slowly started to move lower. He loved how she moved against his touch with complete abandon. He traced and teased her sensitive flesh as she responded more aggressively and the tight clench of muscles signaled another powerful orgasm. His eyes met hers as she drew in a shaky breath.

"Let's go to bed," he said. "I'm not finished."

Chapter 17

Flora woke up and stretched. She bumped Gregory's leg with her own and smiled. Life had certainly been interesting since she had met him. She rolled onto her side and found him staring at her. Trailing one finger over his ribs and down over his hips, she smiled.

"Good morning, beautiful."

"Is that your standard greeting?" she asked.

"You are beautiful, and it is a good morning," Gregory said.

"I'll have no problem getting used to it."

They tried to shower together and failed. Flora's shower just wasn't large enough for the two of them to maneuver. After a few moments of uncomfortableness, Gregory bowed out, and she covered her giggles as he muttered about freezing and definitely having a shower built for two. She soaped and rinsed quickly.

"All done."

"Did you leave me any hot water?" he asked.

"Nope. I figured you would need the cold," Flora said with a wink over her shoulder.

"I should've known. You're too smart and pretty to let the little innocent things go by."

She quickly dressed and made breakfast while Gregory took his shower. Her day was already busy, and on top of it all, she needed to find the appropriate way to thank Shonise. Breakfast was light hearted, and they chatted about their upcoming days. They walked out to Flora's car, and she grinned as she recognized how easy it all felt. A few lingering kisses paused her start to work—not that she minded—and after they came up for air, she stared at him, feeling some kind of tension in the air.

"I talked to Marcus, and he is free to meet tonight," Gregory said.

"Wow. That was quick," she said. "I figured it would take a moment."

"You might as well get to know him sooner. He is an important part of my life, as are you," he said. "I want us to get the introductions done so we can move on with us."

Flora felt a flutter in her stomach and a momentary panic before she smiled at Gregory.

"Okay. Well, I need to get some work done," she said.

"Don't you have your big phone conference today?" Gregory asked her.

"Yes, I do. Thanks for remembering," she said.

"Oh, there is plenty I remember about you," he said. "Especially that freckle under your left knee and the small birthmark in the middle of your back."

Flora blushed, surprising herself.

"I need to get work done, Mr. Bell," she said.

She leaned in and kissed him. Flora made it a point to unlock the car and open the door.

"Have fun with your turtles today."

She got in the car and drove toward Holly and the bookstore to get her day started. Flora found herself engaged in a great conversation with Deanna about working with local, indie authors and how it actually supported the community. Flora was surprised to learn of the camaraderie amongst the authors and chuckled at the good-natured relationships they seemed to have with the bookstore owner. Her day flew by quickly, and when she finally took a break, it was time to meet Marcus.

Flora stood still and pensive as Gregory knocked on Marcus's door. She wasn't sure why she was so surprised that Marcus would also have a cabin on the lake, but she had been. Overall, as she checked in with herself, she realized it was just some mild panic at the prospect of meeting the man responsible for Gregory's pack. The person who had finally allowed Gregory tell her the truth. The door opened, and she was met with a wide smile.

"Gregory, Flora, please come in," Marcus said.

She walked in and took a shaky breath. He seemed nice enough.

Okay, Flora, we asked for this meeting, she said sternly to herself. *Pull it together.*

She sat on the couch as directed and tried not to stare at Marcus. Amazingly, the man looked like any other man on the street. She almost fell into her habit of talking out loud but managed to keep the thoughts in her head.

Right, because Gregory looks like a werewolf. I wonder just how many werepeople I have passed on the street and didn't even know it.

He was about six feet tall, with dark, chocolate skin and eyes to match. His head was the perfect shape to be bald. The thought broke some of the tension, and she giggled just a bit. She wondered how the shifted thing worked, since Gregory had gained a lot of fur. Would Marcus grow fur on his head or not? The notion of a bald headed wolf pushed her laughter louder. She looked away from Marcus and met Gregory's inquisitive stare.

"I will tell you later," she said softly.

"Don't be nervous, Flora Blu," he said. "This is just a friendly meeting."

"I just want to explain a few things before inducting you into our pack," Marcus finished.

Flora sat up stiffly.

"Inducted into the pack?" she squeaked and stared holes into the man sitting next to her. "I don't want to be a werewolf. Gregory, you didn't tell me this was part of the deal."

"You will not be a werewolf, Flora," Marcus said soothingly. "You have to be born one. But I do need to explain to you how our pack works. Being in the know about us means you carry a responsibility for our safety. Part of the way we deal with this is to make you a pack member."

Once her heart calmed back into a manageable beat, she sat back and tried to relax a bit.

"Okay, so what does this induction entail?" Flora asked.

"Only your promises to keep us a secret to everyone, including your family," Marcus said. "Our kind are not treated well by the outside world. There is a lot of misinformation and fear. Be aware that if you do decide to tell someone and they spread information about us, we will take care of it. Permanently."

Flora nodded her head as Marcus gave her a lot of information she would have to process later. However, one statement kept ringing in her head. When he took a pause in his speech, she took a breath and faced him.

"Permanently—as in dead?" she asked.

"Yes," Marcus said with finality. "But only in extreme cases. I don't think you're in that category."

She turned to face Gregory.

"And I would have been *permanently* dealt with had I not accepted Gregory?"

"Not quite. We would have kept you under watch to make sure you didn't betray us."

Flora stared at the man sitting next to her. Scenarios and calculations flew through her mind at top speed. She finally nodded.

"You took a big step in asking to tell me, didn't you?"

She smiled as she looked over at him.

"I knew I loved you enough to fight to keep you in my life," he said. "Consider it a gift."

"Generally, roses are a great gift, but I love you, too, Gregory. I am really glad now that I turned down that job out of state."

"You did?"

"I was going to tell you about it later," she said.

She watched relief cover his face and smiled at him. It had been shocking to hear that her life had been on the line without her ever knowing it. She also realized just what Gregory had done and what it really meant. Flora sat back, more relaxed, and listened to Marcus with certain calm. She found herself proud that Gregory was the next Alpha in line but also relieved that she wasn't going to have to handle pack business herself. She worried a moment what might happen if they decided not to date anymore and then surprised herself by pushing the thoughts aside in favor of planning a long future with him.

"Great. Welcome to the pack, Flora."

She was startled out of her headspace with those words.

"What? That's it? That was my induction?" she asked.

"Would you prefer us to chase you through the woods? I'm sure my friends would be game," Gregory said with a wink.

Flora stared at him until he fidgeted, and Marcus broke into laughter.

"We both know how I feel about nature."

"Good luck, son," Marcus said at the same time as Flora spoke.

Gregory laughed too and stood up to shake Marcus's hand.

"We should go join the party so I can introduce Flora to our friends."

The trio left Marcus's house and much to Flora's relief drove to the party location. She had a momentary panic that she would be required to hike through the woods at night. While she had not worn her wedge shoes, the cute, strappy sandals were not made for any rigorous walking. The walk from the parking lot to the bonfire area was short and the path clear. She looked around, again surprised at how normal everyone looked. She could have never guessed that any of the people there could turn into wolves. She gladly accepted Gregory's hand and stood quietly by his side as he introduced her as his girlfriend. To her surprise, the crowd actually cheered, and she blushed.

"I swear I have had more surprises and incidents of blushing than ever," she whispered to him.

"True, but you have kept the talking to yourself to a minimum so it must be okay," he whispered back.

"You noticed that, huh?" Flora asked him.

"Oh, sweetie, I told you. I notice everything about you."

"Thanks for another blush," she muttered.

They walked through the crowd toward the picnic table holding drinks, and Flora tried to brush off the uneasy feeling of being inspected by the pack. She tried to convince herself that it would take a few times of seeing her before the pack got over their curiosity. However, that was all broken by the intense feeling of fear that ripped up her spine. She looked around and felt her stomach sink.

"Tess, please make Flora feel welcome as a member of the pack," Marcus's voice rang out. "She is with us from now on."

Flora stared at Tess, who stood at the picnic table. She looked at the way the woman clenched the beer bottle and was happy her neck wasn't into the woman's hands.

"Yes, Alpha," Tess said flatly. "Welcome, Flora. Sorry if I didn't recognize you. You are dressed this time."

Flora could feel Gregory stiffen and squeezed his hand. She stared at Tess and then made a point of turning her back to the woman, ignoring the greeting. She then leaned over to grab a beer and as she turned to walk away and held her hand back toward Gregory

"So, Gregory. Where is your infamous crew? I can't wait to meet them."

She could hear the intake of breath from Tess turning into a low growl her as Gregory led her towards the roaring bonfire, near a small group of men who had been watching the whole tense situation unfold. Their smiles were welcoming and she started to relax.

"You should have just taken the fucking job."

The snarled statement made her turn back around and face a woman she was rapidly becoming tired of dealing with.

"Excuse me?"

"I burned a debt to get you a good job offer and out of my damn life," Tess said.

Flora felt a rush of anger and stepped back towards the woman. She had never needed help to get a job in her life, and to think that her interview was due to *her*, sickened Flora. She glared Tess as she walked away from the picnic table and towards the Flora stood. She felt no fear as she sneered at the woman who had changed her life. In anger, words slipped out before she could stop them.

"You just don't when you're not wanted, do you? You don't get it, do you?"

Tess took another step closer to Flora.

"Get what, little girl?"

"You were a distraction. Never wife material, just a blow in the snow," Flora said, standing her ground.

She watched the woman's eyes narrow, but her anger pushed her spine straight.

"How about you try to live your life and stay out of mine," Flora said. "You were never more than a quick lay. When Gregory wanted a relationship, he asked me."

Tess moved much faster than Flora expected and stood before her. She felt Gregory squeeze her hand but dropped his.

"It's okay, Gregory. She needs to learn her place."

"My *place* is Beta. You're just a person in the know," Tess snarled.

"My place is with Gregory," Flora snapped back. "Maybe the pack isn't big enough for two of us."

"Accepted."

Flora felt a ripple of panic run up her spine.

"What?"

"I accept your challenge for my place in the pack," Tess said with a grin that doused Flora in panic.

She looked toward Gregory, who had already placed himself between her and her nemesis.

"You can't challenge her, Tess. Knock off the stupid shit," Gregory said. "Despite you wanting a fight, it's not possible and it's not going to solve anything."

"Actually, I can. You made that possible when you had her inducted," Tess said.

Flora noticed that the people around the bonfire had grown quiet. She was certain it was partially because of her and Tess but also to see what Gregory as their future leader would do. She looked at the resigned expression on his face and stepped back into the conversation.

"Fine. I'll accept your little challenge with some codicils. You do know that means?" she asked Tess and waited for the woman to nod.

"I win, and you not only leave me the hell alone, but you never talk badly about me again to anyone."

Flora was too nervous to feel any sense of victory at the surprised look on Tess's face.

"Okay. And when I win, you will leave forever and forget we exist," Tess said. "Your move."

The silence surrounded Flora, and she looked around, trying to assess how to possibly win against a woman who not only could shift forms but clearly was faster and stronger than she. Her salvation came in the form of a tiny, red, metal object sitting near some chairs next to the bonfire. Flora grabbed it up and turned to face Tess. She grew more irritated by the condescending smile on the woman's face. She held it up and braced herself.

"Really, Flora? By the time you lift that thing up to swing it at me, it will be over," Tess laughed.

Flora thumbed the ring pin off the top of the extinguisher. She held up the hose and squeezed the handles together. As the foam erupted from the nozzle, she counted on the 300 psi of force to keep Tess away from her. Flora watched the foam hit Tess squarely in the face, and the woman fell to her knees, clawing at her throat and face. There was a grim satisfaction in watching the woman writhe on the ground, coughing and sputtering. One simple spray was all it took, but Flora still held the nozzle in her hand and waited to see what Tess would do. Warm hands on her shoulder made her jump.

"Easy, Flora Blu," Gregory's voice rumbled against her back. "You won. I think this was the fastest challenge we have ever seen. You are one resourceful woman. We all expected you to try to hit her with the extinguisher."

"I realized it would've been a stupid plan, Gregory," Flora said. "She would have taken it from me and knocked me unconscious. The best chance I had was to get foam into her mouth and let the chemicals choke the crap out of her."

Flora's attention was drawn back to Tess as she moaned and attempted to stand. The woman was still coughing and spitting out foam. A few others had rushed to her side with washcloths, trying to clean off her face and clear her nose and mouth. While she didn't particularly feel bad for spraying foam at Tess, Flora did not envy the woman the recovery. The foam probably had left frostbite on her face and had the additional side effect of drying out her eyes and nasal passages. It would be a rough few days of healing.

"I think we can all say that Flora won and Tess will abide by the conditions set in the challenge," Marcus said in a clear, strong voice.

The people around the fire and general area murmured consent. Flora sagged against Gregory's chest and took a few moments just to breathe. Her stupid plan of taking on a werewolf and the consequences had just caught up with her. And now that the danger was over, she shook—just a little bit.

"That is done," Gregory said.

"Okay. I do kinda want to spray her again, but Marcus is boss," Flora said, turning to face him. "So it means that we won't ever have to deal with her again?"

"It means Tess will no longer bother you and will not talk poorly about you."

"Okay. I think I could use a drink."

"Let's go grab a beer," Gregory said.

"I don't really like beer. I'm more of a wine girl."

"I'm sure there is something here that you will drink," he said.

Flora smiled when he held up two mini bottles of wine. She would be drinking both.

"My friends have been waiting to meet you.

Flora turned to face him and didn't mind when he pulled her into a kiss in front of everyone. She pulled back and gave him a satisfied smile.

"Hopefully none of your friends will want to challenge me," she said.

"After the show you just gave them? Flora Blu, I do believe that even Nathaniel will behave."

Flora laughed and went to meet Gregory's friends.

Chapter 18

"Mama, Daddy, this is Gregory," Flora said, releasing a shaky breath. "My boyfriend."

She faced Gregory and tried out a smile. She felt like she was going to throw up. He poked his head out of the bathroom with a toothbrush in his mouth.

"Hmmm?"

"Do I sound as scared as I feel?"

"Mhummu, hmmmm."

"Great. I guess I get to be nervous, then. This is terrible," Flora said.

Flora resumed pacing before getting an answer from him.

"You took on Tess and won, but you are nervous to introduce me to your parents?" he asked.

She fixed him with a stare and then burst out in nervous laughter.

"Well, I guess when you put it like that…"

She ran her sweaty palms down the side of her skirt. Gregory stepped out of the bathroom and took her breath away. He was dressed in khakis and a navy blue polo shirt. Flora ran her hand down his arm and leaned in for a kiss. His touch fortified her, and before things got too hot, she pulled away from him and smiled.

"Let's go do this. I did just take on a werewolf and win."

Flora led the way out of her apartment and outside. Despite Gregory's attempt at keeping the atmosphere light and tension free, she grew quiet on the too quick walk to the restaurant. As Gregory opened the door for her, she gave him a quick smile and then grabbed his hand. It felt odd to her to feel so possessive of him, but she wanted to make a statement. After the whole incident with Tess, she knew something in her had changed. With her held high, she easily navigated through the restaurant and walked up to her parents as they sat.

"Hi, Mama. Hi, Daddy," she said. "This is my boyfriend, Gregory."

Flora felt a flush rise up her neck into her cheeks at the look from her mother. No matter how old she got, she would always be easily cowed by the woman. However, she stood tall and waited. To her absolute surprise, her mother gave a welcoming smile. Her father rose, gave her a hug, and then shook Gregory's hand. She sat while Gregory was shaking her mother's hand as he gave her a slight bow. Despite the urge to look around for alien pods, Flora tried to relax. She knew her parents would like Gregory and be happy for her. At least, that was the mantra she kept running in her mind.

"I'm glad you finally decided to introduce us to your friend, Flora," her mother said and smiled at her. "I expected to have to chase you down."

Flora got a sinking feeling and fixed her napkin in her lap. Three times.

"Mama saw you at the dry cleaner's a few weeks back, but you left before she could turn around to greet you," her father said.

"Of course you did," Flora mumbled.

"Keen powers of observation apparently run in the family," Gregory said with a grin.

Lunches were quickly ordered, and Flora tried to think of stimulating things to entertain her parents with so they wouldn't pry. The tactic lasted only until the lunches were delivered and the waiter disappeared.

"How did you meet Flora?" her mother asked.

Flora idly wondered if she should have prepared Gregory for an interrogation by her parents, but she didn't know what to expect. He was the first man she had brought to meet them, the first one she was serious about. Truth be told, she was still relieved that her parents had not pressed her about running away from the dry cleaner's any more.

"I met her at the turtle pond at For-Mar," Gregory answered.

Flora smiled as her parents looked at Gregory with skepticism, then at each other, and finally at her.

"You went to For-Mar?" her father asked. "Willingly?"

"Yes, Daddy," Flora said with a grin.

She made it a point to take a huge bite of her sandwich to stay the next inevitable questions.

"You did realize it was an arboretum and nature preserve?" her mother asked.

"Yes, Mama," she said. "They hired me."

"You are a programmer. I'm not quite seeing nature and computers coming together," her mother said.

Flora noticed that Gregory's grin widened and sighed.

"For-Mar hired me to create a database to catalogue their Eastern box turtles. Before you ask, yes, I knew I would have to be in nature, but it was a job and Flora Blu Designs doesn't turn down jobs," she said. "Gregory saved me from being ravaged by piranhas as I set up equipment. That's how we met."

"Piranhas are in the Amazon basin, dear," her mother corrected.

Flora didn't roll her eyes but couldn't manage not to sound indignant as she offered an explanation.

"Well, Michigan must have some new, invasive variety, because as I stood in the water, fish nibbled at me."

As she met her parents' amazed expressions, Flora launched into the tame parts of her dating experiences, aside from the whole werewolf challenge. Gregory pitched in with details about their nature date, and her parents laughed good naturedly.

"I can't believe you managed to convince my daughter to have a picnic," her father said. "Outside even."

"Daddy, I do go to family reunions, and they are outside," Flora protested.

"Yes, but the entire family knows how you feel about it," her mother said. "Remember the year you brought the sonic bug repellers?"

Flora could feel the heat of Gregory's stare but refused to face him. She smiled and grabbed the menu to choose her desert. She had just decided on a bowl of fruit when she heard a voice that froze her.

"Brother and Sister Blu, how lovely to see you here with young Sister Blu and her date."

Flora put down the menu and met Pastor Jenkins's smile.

"Mr. Bell," the pastor greeted and offered his hand. "I do hope this means our church family will be graced with your presence soon."

"I certainly plan to," Gregory said.

Flora couldn't stop the blush but managed to smile back at the pastor nonetheless.

"Pastor Jenkins, how lovely to see you here," she said.

"I'm glad to see you as well, Sister Blu," Pastor said.

Flora felt the blush burn brighter as the pastor related their last meeting to her parents. She stared at Gregory, willing him to come up with an excuse or something to have them leave early. He failed to get the hint as he was busy laughing with her parents and her pastor. After a few moments, the pastor left them to resume their lunch, but the jovial atmosphere remained. Flora finally gave in and relaxed. She joined in with the laughter, and they finished lunch on a high note.

Flora exhaled a relieved breath. She had finished the database earlier in the week and was told she would need to present the data to the specialist on staff and two board members. She was glad to have finished the project and was proud to be able to present her work.

However, she still got nervous in meetings. Thankfully, she had been kept busy with new projects coming in. Two of the pack members were small business owners who needed their own webstores, and her church had hired her not only to make a website but also create a special chat forum for the teens. She had seen Gregory only once over the past four days and wanted to spend more time with him.

She smoothed her tangerine shirt and stared in the mirror. She was glad she had turned down the job offer. Not just because it was Tess that had pulled the strings, but because she stayed true to her business objective of keeping her company in Flint. What she had not told Gregory was that her big conference call had been with the National Zoo in Washington, D.C., who also had wanted a turtle database set up.

Initially, she had been excited. She was thrilled at the prospect, but the details decided it wasn't for her. They wanted her as a contract specialist, but they also expected her to move to the D.C. area for at least six months to get everything set up and train staff to maintain the database. While the paycheck was pretty, the relocation was not. If she wasn't willing to move an hour away to Ann Arbor, there was no way she was going to D.C. for six months. The fact that her refusal to move had pissed Tess off—pure bonus. As she looked again at her face in the mirror, she smiled.

"Still the same Flora," she breathed and then laughed. "Yeah, right. Just the same ole' Flora who hates nature and is dating a werewolf."

Her pep talk stilled her nerves, and she got ready to go to For-Mar to turn in the project. Along with the digital database, Flora had printed a book that contained not only pictures of each turtle but a diagram write-up, explaining the shell pattern information. She tried to call Gregory on her way over, but it went to voicemail. She had hoped that he would have been able to talk her down a few pegs.

She walked into the visitor's center and smiled.

"Hi, Ginny," she said. "I have a meeting…"

"Back room on the right," Ginny smiled. "Even though you're done, don't be a stranger. I'll be sad not to see you."

Flora nodded and walked down the short hall. She grabbed the handle and then took a deep breath. She pulled the doors open and walked into the room as if she owned it. Only practice in dancing around in heels gave her the ability not to trip over the threshold in shock at seeing Gregory sitting at the head of the table. He looked very much the professional in a dress shirt and tie with a man on either side of him. His slow, deliberate wink at her settled her nerves, to her amazement. She smiled at each of the men at the table and then launched into her presentation before her nerves took over.

"So, the database program was successful, and you have at least eighty healthy turtles in the pond. Probably another dozen or so that were camera shy. Thank you for this amazing opportunity to work for the Genesee County Parks."

The men stood up and thanked her, much handshaking was done, and then she was alone in the room with Gregory.

"Nicely done, Flora Blu," he said, smiling down at her.

"You could have told me you were going to be at the meeting, Gregory," she said, wrinkling her nose.

"Being the only testudinologist at the park, I rather assumed you knew I would be here," he said with an easy grin. "I do run the turtle programs."

She joined his laughter.

"So, how about you buy this girl some dinner?" she asked.

"Weren't you the one with the big payday?" he teased.

"Gregory, that is the business account," she said loftily. "I planned for this to be pleasure."

"By all means, then, Ms. Blu. It will be my honor to take you to dinner, on one condition."

Flora raised an eyebrow and poked him in the chest.

"Don't tell me about any more conditions. The last few have been pretty life changing," she said. "And no, it cannot be a picnic in nature."

"No, I was going to ask that you allow me the honor of cooking for you," he said. "I want to have a cookout with my friends, so they really get to know you. Last time they saw you was under pretty dramatic circumstances."

"Can I bring Shonise?"

"Will she bleach my lake?"

Flora laughed and poked him again.

"She was only going to do that if you turned out to be an asshole, but since you were just a wolf—otherwise known as a recovering alcoholic—I highly doubt she will bleach your lake."

She wasn't the least chagrined as Gregory joined her in laughter. They walked out of the meeting room and to her car, still chuckling. Flora turned to face him.

"I am glad I took this assignment. It led me right to you," she said. "I wasn't even looking for romance."

"Neither was I, but out of the blue, you showed up."

She groaned at the pun on her name but allowed herself to be pulled into a hug.

"I cannot imagine my life without you," he said.

"Now you don't have to," Flora said. "I love you, Gregory Bell."

"And I love you, Flora Blu."

They kissed until kids in a nearby bus started making noises at them. Flora floated away with the promise of the evening party and a relationship that would only continue to grow.

About The STEAM Series

Dear Readers,

Most of you have heard of the STEM subjects- Science—Technology—Engineering—Mathematics.

However there has been a push from those in The Arts and Humanities to remember that arts and creativity are part of the process that makes things go. While educationally encouraging more women to explore the STEM subject is a great start, the critical process of creativity and innovation is missing.

STEAM is an educational approach to learning that uses Science, Technology, Engineering, the Arts and Mathematics as starting guide for critical thinking and discourse.

I chose to highlight this because you will find the women in this series, to be smart and savvy in their fields, but definitely creative when it comes to living a world where the paranormal is real.

Happy Reading!

JFF

About the Author

Jennifer Fisch- Ferguson has been writing and publishing fantasy stories since 2003. Publishing credits include writing contests and self-published novels and two separate series under consideration by agents.

She attended the Eastern Michigan University and graduated with a B.A in African American History and promptly went to work with AmeriCorps on a literary initiative. She went to the University of Michigan and got her Master's degree in Public Administration in 2008 and while she finished writing her thesis, also got a Masters in English – Composition and Rhetoric in 2009. She received her PhD at Michigan State University in the field of Professional Writing and Digital Rhetorics. She has been teaching collegiate and community writing classes since 2003 and loves the variety and inspiration her students bring.

She writes urban fantasy, paranormal romance, and young adult urban fantasy. She is excitedly expanding her ever developing world and looks forward to the new adventures waiting to be written.

See more at:

AuthorJFF.com

https://www.facebook.com/ETM.JFF

Sneak Peek: The STEAM Series Book 2
Moonstruck

Chapter One

Siona Carter looked away from her computer screen and squinted at the clock on the wall. She deliberately kept it where she would need to look up to see it so she could refresh her eyes from the up close viewing of her computer screen. As she rotated her neck, her thick short coils of hair tickled her nape and she grinned. After years of not being sure just what to do with it, she had finally settled on working with the natural texture of her curls and embracing it. She grew tired of being chemically burned three or four times a year, just to keep her hair straight. Her dark hair set off equally dark brown eyes that were just big enough to look intrigued but not constantly surprised. She stood proud at five foot nine, and after seeing a terrifying video on the detriments of high heels on the foot bones, she happily switched flats.

She walked through the doors of the Hayden Planetarium and felt her heart speed up just a bit. She had been working with there for eighteen months and it still thrilled her to go to her job every day. She had loved astronomy from a young age; despite living in Manhattan and barely being able to make out the stars from the city burn. Perhaps, it would be better to say she was obsessed about the stars. She had learned to drive only because her parents reminded her that it was only a short drive away from the city to be able to see her beloved night sky. Of course it became moot point, because instead of asking for a car as a graduation gift, she had requested a telescope.

Not any little off the shelf scope, she proudly owned the Dobsian Obsession. Fifteen inches of precision-cut quality mirrors in a mounting that gave her the crispest images and lacked the distortion thinners mirrors often showed. For her it was the obvious choice of presents to receive. Prior to the telescope request, her parents had thought it a phase she was going through. Instead, Siona majored in Astrophysics and planned to go to graduate school after some research to add to her CV. Then she filled out an internship application, with no hopes of ever really making it.

The summer experience resulted in her being offered a full blown research and development job at the Hayden had been a dream come true. Granted she had only seen Dr. de Grasse Tyson a handful of times, and she doubted he knew who she was, it was still exciting to be in the same facility with the man who had made her field cool with the public masses. Though she did get tired of people asking her what she did for a living. The very long answer was that she used a lot of the principles of physics and mathematics to learn more about the universe. Her particular position was to gather data on a parameter study of the possibility of tidally triggered disc instability, which she believed could theoretically could lead to enhanced planetesimal formation in the outer regions of the protoplanetary disc and could therefore be relevant for the existence of Neptune. She was leading up to writing a scientific paper to present to the field. The short answer, how and possibly why Neptune existed.

While she loved her job, she did want to finish her degree and maybe even teach. However, it was expensive to go to graduate school and she had needed a brain break.

Seven hours later, Siona stretched and stood up. Her office remained a chilly sixty-eight degrees, which against the summer New York heat, was perfectly fine. Her computer chimed and her eyes flicked over to the screen. There was a group email reminding everyone that their secretary Lisa would be going out on maternity leave and to chip in for the party on Friday. Siona tried not to shudder, she loathed work parties. They were too loud and chaotic and she had never quite fit in. Her section of research and design collaborated with the Dish in Australia. Which meant the not-quite-but-really mandatory work parties forced her to be awake and more social at a time she was not comfortable with. She hoped that donating fifty dollars with a lame excuse would get her out of the celebration.

Her phone buzzed against her leg. She took out the phone with a slight panic. The only calls allowed through during work were from her parents. She spoke with her mother on the days containing a 'T' at eight in the morning religiously, so a call ringing in at six am made her worry. She tried to push the panic back and sound reasonably calm as she answered.

"Mom?" she asked.

"You're taking your break, yes?"

"Yes. What's wrong, Mom?" she asked.

"Nothing, Siona. I just needed to talk to you and I know you take a break now," her mother said.

Siona scaled back the panic a few notches. Her mother's voice was calm and collected. Not to mention she was right, Siona's break schedule was absolutely predictable. Then again, why not wait to call at eight?

"Okay, did you have a problem sleeping?"

"Oh, my worried child, relax. I am often up at six a.m. retired or not, it's hard to break a thirty year work habit of getting up early."

Siona nodded at the phone and grabbed her Bluetooth. Usually her six a.m. break meant grabbing an apple or pear, and walking twenty laps around her department. Twenty laps was exactly a mile, and with all the sitting she did on a nightly basis Siona was determined not to have varicose veins at a young age. She grimaced as she figured the eating part of her routine would have to wait. She left her office and began her walk.

"What has you calling me so early, if it's not an emergency?" she asked.

"I wanted to let you know that we have plans this summer," her mother said.

"Oh, good. Are you and Dad going to finally take the vacation you wanted?"

"We have a family reunion this year we plan to attend," her mother said.

"Great. I think you will have a lot of fun. Are you going to drive or fly?"

"We plan to drive; you still have three weeks of unused vacation, right?"

Siona almost tripped as her mother's question caught up with her. She was glad for the empty corridor to spare her the embarrassment and continued on her walk.

"What does my accrued vacation time have anything to do with your vacation?" she asked cautiously.

"Siona. Did you miss the part where I said we were going to a family reunion?"

"Oh, you mean *we,* as in the whole family," Siona said flatly.

"And this is why you graduated with honors," her mother quipped.

"Thanks Mom," Siona said drily. "When is the blessed event?"

"August, I gave you three months' notice," her mother said.

Siona could picture the smug smile her mother wore on the other end. As she ran through a list of excuses, she realized there weren't any. As her mother well knew, she had not actually taken a leave since starting her job. The Hayden was more than generous with time off for her department; however, Siona hadn't taken used the days because she saw no need. Her job fascinated her and she loved what she did. She had apparently made a huge mistake in telling her mother about the vacation time- since now it was being used against her.

"August, okay. If you can just text me the dates, I will put in my request."

"Don't sound so excited, Si," her mother laughed. "You have enjoyed the family reunions so far. It's been four years since our last visit, so it's time."

Siona again nodded to the empty hall. Despite being an only child and used to peace and quiet, she had found her extended family to be warm and welcoming when they had gone before. There would be music, storytelling, more food than the imagination could conjure and hordes of family members. The family reunions always spanned the better part of two weeks and alternated between a northern and southern location every two years.

"Where are we at this year?

"Burton, Michigan."

"Oh, I should have figured. How long has it been since you've been home, Mom?" Siona asked.

Her memories of her mother's hometown were pretty vague. The most she knew is that it was a factory city. The freeways seemed to go on forever, but the good part was no traffic. And the donuts; even after eight years Siona's mouth watered with the remembrance of the nutty donuts and made a mental note to ask her mother about the place. She continued to chat with her mom for her twenty minute break and promised to have her vacation request turned in before she left.

Siona went back to her lab and dove back into her work. She was deep into her numerical data when her computer chimed. Another email reminder about the baby shower for the morning crew had made its way into her mailbox. She sighed and began to close down for the day. Her phone chirped and she sighed when she saw the text from her mom. If she didn't fill out the request form, her mother had threatened to. On her way out she stopped by the HR department.

"Hey Tony," she said brightly as she walked up to the secretary.

"Hello, Siona. How was your night?" he asked.

"Fascinating as ever, but I will spare you my ramble and details you don't really want," she said with a smile.

She waited patiently as Tony took a long sip of coffee and sighed.

"See? I love that about you," he said. "You don't make me pretend to care and leave me to drink my coffee."

"You still owe me a cup from the little place on West 81st."

Being a third shift worker meant being off schedule with most of the people around her. However one thing was consistent in the Universe- coffee was the nectar of life. Tony was one of the few people who respected the differences of schedules. He grinned and waved away her reminder.

"Okay, tomorrow," he said. "Now, what can I help you with?"

"Well, here is $50 for Lisa's baby shower. When is it again?" she asked.

Tony laughed and took the money. "You've been practicing. That almost sounded like genuine interest. It's Friday at three; so sadly, you will miss the shower by a good seven hours."

Siona blessed her four day — ten hour work schedule for giving her a reprieve and tried not to look too relieved.

"Okay. I also need a vacation request form," she said.

Tony's eyebrows rose, but he said nothing as he found the appropriate form and handed it to her. She quickly scribbled out her request and turned the paper back over to him. She watched him scan it. He seemed too interested in the form.

"Thank you, Siona," he said a bit too eagerly.

"What?" she asked cautiously.

"Nothing, you're all set. I'll turn this in and you should hear back no later than end of the week," Tony said still smiling widely.

"No, there's more to it than that," her eyes narrowed. "You're grinning like Christmas just came early."

"Well, there might be a pool of bets about when or if certain staff members will use their vacation."

"So, what you are saying is there is no way this vacation request will be denied?" she asked in a forlorn tone.

"Why would you want your vacation denied?" Tony asked.

"Did you not see the reason line where I wrote 'family vacation'?" she asked.

Tony nodded and took another sip of his coffee.

"That I did, but, I also happen to know the two people who straddle your vacation dates are in HR," he said. "Go enjoy your family and remember that you get to come back to your quiet lab."

"You are no help what so ever," she grumbled. "You were supposed to save me from having to take this extended vacation."

"Where are you going? It can't possibly be that bad," he said.

"Michigan."

"And you are complaining why? Take your telescope and view the stars from a different latitude and longitude. I'm sure there might even be a planetarium or two around you to play with," Tony mocked her. "And in case you ever wondered, this is why we take bets on when you scientists will actually use your vacation time."

Siona rolled her eyes at him.

"I can really count on going?" she asked. "There is no way to get out of this?"

"Oh, yes. You are going. The pot is pretty good," he said. "I don't suppose I can talk you into talking all three weeks?"

"You plan to cut me in?"

"And promote gambling at work? I work in HR, I couldn't possibly do that," Tony said in mock outrage.

Siona gave a general sigh of disgust and was about to leave when a tall woman with perfectly coiffed hair walked into the office. Tony greeted her with enthusiasm.

"Look Kim, Siona turned in a request for vacation."

"When? Please tell me August," Kim said, shooting Siona a bright smile.

"You got it; the second and third week," Tony said. "Maybe you could convince her to take that extra week? I mean, when else is she ever going to use it?"

Siona sighed deeply at the exuberance in his voice. There was no disguising the glee coming from her co-workers and she knew her vacation would be a sure thing. She wondered if it might be possible to get a really nasty summer cold, just before the reunion which would force her to stay home.

"Come to Mama!" Kim said.

Siona watched in horror as Tony handed the paper over, and Kim scrawled her signature at the bottom. She then ripped off the carbon bottom and handed it to Siona.

"Have a lovely trip, Siona," she said. "I gave you the extra week anyhow."

"You two should be ashamed of yourselves," Siona muttered. "You were supposed to be my excuse not to have to go on a family vacation."

"Siona, really. Everyone needs to take a break from work," Kim said. "You have been here for eighteen months, two weeks and three days. You have never called out sick, taken any personal days, nor vacation. If it weren't against the rules, I would tell your mother you could take the entire month of August off with no problem."

"Oh yes, I'm sure my well-being is the reason for the rapid approval," Siona grumbled.

She left the office shaking her head at the laughter that followed her out the door. She walked out of the planetarium and made her way to the subway and home. Siona knew that the summer would pass rapidly fast to spite her. Fatigue hit her as soon as she sat in her favorite rocking chair.

Siona decided to forgo her morning ritual of looking at Sirius and instead crawled into bed with her ebook reader and started to read. She yawned as she reread the last paragraph; twice, then gave up and put her device down. Soon the din of the city would rise to full blown noise, and it would serve as her lullaby as she went to sleep.